Mysterious Robbery on the Utah Plains

Crossway Books for Young People by Stephen Bly

THE NATHAN T. RIGGINS WESTERN ADVENTURE SERIES
The Dog Who Would Not Smile
Coyote True
You Can Always Trust a Spotted Horse
The Last Stubborn Buffalo in Nevada
Never Dance with a Bobcat
Hawks Don't Say Goodbye

THE LEWIS AND CLARK SQUAD ADVENTURE SERIES
Intrigue at the Rafter B Ranch
The Secret of the Old Rifle
Treachery at the River Canyon
Revenge on Eagle Island
Danger at Deception Pass
Hazards of the Half-Court Press

RETTA BARRE'S OREGON TRAIL
The Lost Wagon Train
The Buffalo's Last Stand
The Plain Prairie Princess

ADVENTURES ON THE AMERICAN FRONTIER
Daring Rescue at Sonora Pass
Dangerous Ride Across Humboldt Flats
Mysterious Robbery on the Utah Plains

Adventures on the American Frontier ★ Book 3

Mysterious Robbery
on the Utah Plains

Stephen Bly

CROSSWAY BOOKS

A DIVISION OF
GOOD NEWS PUBLISHERS
WHEATON, ILLINOIS

Mysterious Robbery on the Utah Plains

Copyright © 2003 by Stephen Bly

Published by Crossway Books
              a division of Good News Publishers
              1300 Crescent Street
              Wheaton, Illinois 60187

Cover design: David LaPlaca

Cover illustration: Vito DiAngi

First printing 2003

Printed in the United States of America

ISBN 1-58134-473-2

Library of Congress Cataloging-in-Publication Data
Bly, Stephen A., 1944 -
   Mysterious robbery on the Utah plains / Stephen Bly.
      p. cm. — (Adventures on the American Frontier ; bk. 3)
   Summary: On the eve of the ceremonies to mark the completion of
the transcontinental railroad in 1869, gunmen hide a mysterious pack-
age at the Hopewells' bakery, which nearly causes the family to lose
their business until they discover that God has had an exciting plan for
them all along.
   ISBN 1-58134-473-2 (TPB)
   [1. Railroads—Fiction. 2. Frontier and pioneer life—Fiction.
3. Robbers and outlaws—Fiction. 4. Christian life—Fiction.] I. Title.
II. Series.
PZ7.B6275My   2003
[Fic]—dc22   2003011592

DP		13	12	11	10	09	08	07	06	05	04	03
15	14	13	12	11	10	9	8	7	6	5	4	3	2	1

*"Pure religion and undefiled
before God and the Father is this,
To visit the fatherless and widows
in their affliction,
and to keep himself unspotted from the world."*
James 1:27 (KJV)

Author's Note

As a young man, I worked on a ranch where every other section of land (640 acres) was owned by the Southern Pacific Railroad. I knew the stories since childhood of how the railroad amassed great quantities of land as they laid the iron rails that joined east and west. I often passed the signs that marked the site of the Mussel Slough Tragedy (May 11, 1880), which was one of the darkest days in the history of the railroad in the West.

Yet, as a third-generation Westerner, I understood that without such incentives, the railroads would not have been built for another fifty years. It was, as many writers have claimed, "the giveaway that gave America the West." A transcontinental railroad was perhaps the greatest industrial achievement of the nineteenth century.

A marvel in engineering, determination, and just plain hard work, this advancement in transportation was almost incomprehensible at the time. Instead of four to six grueling months in a covered wagon, a person could board the express in Omaha and be in San Francisco in four days. Virginia Reed was thirteen years old when she survived the incredible ordeal of the Donner party's crossing of the Sierra Nevada in 1846. At the age of thirty-six she could have made the same trip in ninety-six hours.

Most people at the time knew they were making history. The events on the Utah Plains at Promontory Point on May 10, 1869, were chronicled in every newspaper in America. Many from east and west came to witness the great event. Others came simply because they needed the money a railroad camp would provide.

The Hopewells were one such family.

Stephen Bly,
Winchester, Idaho
Spring of 2003

ONE

Friday, May 7, 1869, west of Ogden, Utah Territory

The fourteen-year-old stuck his head behind the canvas flap that served as the front door of the ten-by-twelve white canvas side-wall tent. "I'm down to my last pan full, and I've got 'em standin' in line clean down to the railroad tracks!" Sweat drenched the tight collar of Alexander Hopewell's white cotton shirt.

Behind him two dozen men, dressed in everything from linen suits to denim coveralls, milled around between the tent shops, licking lips covered, like everything else, with fine yellow dust.

Mrs. Napoleon Hopewell glanced up from the giant cast-iron frying pan and tried to brush her blonde hair off her forehead with the back of her hand. "Sell this last pan full; then hang up the Closed sign."

Alex turned to look at the sunken eyes of a thin Irish laborer who stood behind a fat, red-nosed gambler. "They'll be heartbroken, Mama. They've been pinin' for a Mrs. Hopewell doughnut."

"No man ever died from lack of a doughnut. Tell them no more until daybreak tomorrow. If we don't let the stove and the cook rest a bit, there won't be any then."

She rubbed the small of her back and stood up straight just a little at a time.

"Wait until tomorrow? There might be a riot out here over these last nine," Alex worried.

She stepped over to the tent pole and peeked at the tiny mirror that dangled on a nail. "You want me to tell them?"

Alex tugged at his shirt collar. "Yes, ma'am."

He watched as his mother dried her hands on the apron. Her blue eyes were wide, round, and tired. Her round cheeks were reddened from the hot stove. She set her hair in her combs and tugged off the apron, laying it on a fifty-pound sack of flour. Then she strolled toward him.

Alex held the flap open. *Lord, Mama works too hard, and there is nothing I can do about it. She drives herself, and it scares me. I try to do what I can, but it's never enough.*

Mrs. Hopewell pushed out into north Utah's early May sunlight. She smelled like sugar and rose water perfume and stood several inches shorter than Alex.

"Boys," she called out, her hands on her full hips, "we've got nine more doughnuts. I'll sell one each to the next nine men. Then we're closed 'til tomorrow. Sorry."

"Mrs. Hopewell, I'll pay you double for all nine!" a man in a silk top hat shouted.

"And I'll pay triple," a deep voice in the back boomed.

She studied the man at the back. "Mr. Mudd, you look quite nice with a haircut and your beard trimmed."

"Thank ya, Daisy. Do I get them last nine bear signs?"

"These are doughnuts, not bear signs. Each one has

a hole, and, no, you don't get any at all. One each to the next nine men in line. You heard me."

Alex stood beside her with the last batch of doughnuts.

The big man scooted closer. "You'd turn down a big cash profit, Mrs. Hopewell?"

"Mr. Mudd, these boys have been waitin' a long time." She turned to the hollow-eyed Irishman. "Sean, how long have you had to wait?"

He licked his narrow, tight lips. "Close to two hours, Mrs. Hopewell."

"You see? Sean deserves one of them. I advertise skillet-fresh doughnuts for ten cents, and I won't sell them for more. Besides, that's twice what I get paid for them in Ogden City." She folded her arms and rubbed her shoulders.

"Will you marry me, Widow Hopewell?" Mudd shouted.

The men laughed and whistled.

Daisy Hopewell handed out the doughnuts with wooden tongs to the next nine men as Alex collected a dime from each of them. Then she waved the wooden tongs at the bearded man. "Montana Mudd, you ask that same thing of every unmarried woman in northern Utah."

"That ain't true, Daisy." He pulled off his new bowler and held it in his hand. "I avoid saying it to the Mormon Saints and them that can't cook."

She reached out and took the arm of his wool suit coat. "And all of those other women turned you down?"

"Yeah, don't that beat all?" He patted her hand. "Maybe I'm too handsome for them."

"No, I don't think that's it." She laughed and released his arm.

"Shoot, Daisy, you didn't have to answer me so quick," he hooted.

The men dispersed in all directions through the haphazard tents that made up a small village. Mrs. Hopewell hiked to the barrels that formed the outside counter in front of the tent. "Montana, I thought you'd be up in the high mountains by now."

"I reckoned I'd wait until tomorrow to see me some history."

Alex pointed south. "The railroad line was finished yesterday except that last section. I heard they're waiting around for Mr. Stanford and Mr. Durant to show up."

Mudd shoved on his hat. "And all them newspaper reporters. I figure to get myself in a photograph. Wouldn't that be swell? Montana Mudd at the drivin' of the golden spike. A hundred years from now, they'll say, 'Who is that fine-lookin' gentleman in the crisp beaver bowler?'"

"A coast-to-coast railroad is amazing," Mrs. Hopewell agreed. "I wish my Napoleon could have lived to see the day. My, how he wanted to drive a train all the way to California."

Mudd pulled off his hat again and held it over his heart. "He was a good man, Daisy. I ain't sure why the Lord takes fine men like your Napoleon and leaves ol' reprobates like me here on this earth," he mumbled. "I reckon it don't seem fair."

"Mama says it's 'cause men like you still need a lot of work. Daddy was all fit and ready for heaven," Alex blurted out.

"Hah," Mudd roared. "Your mama is a smart

woman, son. I don't surmise I have a mansion waitin' in heaven."

"You could, you know," she said.

"She's not only smart, but she's the best doughnut cook west of St. Louis."

"Alex, do you notice how some men divert the attention away from spiritual matters?"

"Yep, Mama, I noticed that, but he also limited your cookin' to merely the best out west."

"I ain't been east of St. Louis, and so I can't honestly evaluate the rest of the country," Mudd bellowed. "I'll be back in the mornin', Daisy. Are you goin' to preach at me?"

"I just might, Mr. Mudd."

"A fair trade for one of your doughnuts," he said.

Alex and his mother watched Montana Mudd stomp back through the tents strung out on the north side of the railroad tracks. He handed her the nine dimes. "We made thirty-two dozen and gave away or ate eighteen doughnuts. That makes $36.60 just today."

"Sounds almost sinful, doesn't it?"

"It's nice to make a profit like that. Mama, you had to work hard. You earned it."

"So did you, honey. I couldn't do it without my Alex."

"We'd better get them pans washed."

She folded her arms across her chest and surveyed the camp. "I'm still waiting for Cyrus to get back with the water."

Alex unfastened his shirt collar and plucked up his slouch hat and crammed it on. "I'll go find him. Do you want me to take King?"

She gathered several empty pans off the counter in front of the tent. "No, he can stay and help me straighten up."

"If I take him with me and you don't have any water, there'll be nothin' for you to do but lay on the cot and take a little rest until I get back," Alex suggested.

A smile softened her face. "Darlin', you're a jewel. Take little brother and don't hurry." She handed him two dimes. "There's a nickel for you, King, and Cyrus too."

"What can I get you, Mama?"

She rubbed her chin. "I would like an orange. But don't you pay more than a nickel for one. I've never eaten a dime orange in my life and don't intend to now."

Ten-year-old redheaded Darius Hopewell tramped around the corner of the tent with an arm of sage firewood. "Are we closed up?" he asked.

"Yep. Now you and me have to go find Cyrus," Alex announced.

"I'm tired," Darius protested. "Do I have to?"

"Mama gave us a nickel each to spend."

"I'm not all that tired."

The Utah Plains at the north end of Promontory Point were no more than a flat, treeless basin with widely scattered sage and sparse clumps of grass. To the southwest, the noontime sun reflected off Gunnison Bay of the Great Salt Lake and made it sparkle like some mythical sea. The railroad camp was nothing more than a tent town stretched in no particular pattern between the Promontory and North Promontory Mountains.

There was only one reason they had all congregated

there. After May 8 Alex figured the reason and the people would be gone.

"Where's Cyrus?" Darius asked.

"He went to get water." Alex clutched his brother's hand and led him through a crowd of lounging railroad workers. "I reckon he's by the water wagons."

"He's been gone over an hour," Darius said.

"Cyrus likes to visit."

"Mama says he's as good at visiting as Daddy." Darius scurried to keep up.

"And Daddy was surely the best."

"What am I the best at, Alex?"

"Why, at eatin' doughnuts for one thing. That's why ever'one calls you King."

"I mean, besides that."

"You're only ten. You don't have to be the best at anything."

"How old does a boy have to be—to be the best at something?"

Alex looped his arm around his youngest brother's shoulder. "Now look at me. I'm fourteen. What am I the best at?"

"Mama says you're the best salesman, the best reader, and the best shot in the family."

"I guess you have to be about twelve to be best at something."

"Cyrus is the best at meetin' new people and what else?"

"He's the best dreamer and inventor," Alex replied. "Here's the water tanks. I don't see him."

A tall, long-bearded man with slouch hat and a brass-framed Winchester 1866 carbine lounged at the back of a huge water wagon. Alex meandered over to him. "Cecil, have you seen my brother?"

"Howdy, Alexander. Howdy, King. Cyrus was by here about an hour ago. He shoved your buckets back there under the wagon and took off to the west. Said he'd be right back."

"Did he bring you a doughnut?" Alex asked.

"Yep. Tell your mama it was mighty tasty."

"We'll go find him and then come back for some water."

"I ain't goin' nowhere. This crowd is gettin' bigger and bigger." Cecil pointed with his carbine. "If they get anxious for fresh water, I'll have trouble."

Alex and King stomped past the crowded row of tents west of the water wagon. King tugged on his sleeve. "How come they need a man with a gun at the water wagon?"

"So people don't steal the water."

"Water ought to be free," King mumbled.

"Not when they have to haul it twenty miles. Where do you think Cyrus went to? The Central Pacific side? Or the Union Pacific side?"

"Central Pacific. He's been workin' on a cowcatcher that would remove snow and turn it into drinking water," King reported. "They need more help with snow on the Central Pacific side."

They traipsed by a tent twice the size of any of the others. "They have a piano in there," King hollered.

"Yep."

"Can we go listen to it?"

"Nope," Alex said.

"What are they sellin'?"

"Sin."

"Can we just peek in the flap?"

"Nope. Mama would tan our hides."

"She don't ever whip you—just me and Cyrus."

"I had my share when I was young. Let's check out that tent over there."

"What are they sellin'?"

"California produce."

"I don't want no radishes. I want some candy," King pouted.

Boards were stretched across barrels to make outdoor shelves. They were stacked with apples, round melons, long green squash, bunches of radishes, and big yellow onions.

A tall girl, with long, straight blonde hair parted in the middle and a burgundy gingham dress, stood by the tent flap as they walked up.

"Hi," she smiled. "Are you new here?"

"Ever'body is new here," Alex mumbled. "Do you have any oranges?"

"We've been here since yesterday. Yes, we have peaches, strawberries, and oranges in the back. Daddy says they're too expensive to set out here. Someone might steal them."

"We've been here for two weeks," King reported.

"You haven't either," she snapped. "The tracks haven't been here for two weeks."

"We moved in with the grading crew," Alex said. "Are the oranges any good?"

She folded her arms. "You think we'd sell lousy oranges?"

"No, I don't guess so." He scratched the back of his neck. "How much are they?"

"Do you have a shop, or do you work for the railroad?" she questioned.

"Mama sells doughnuts," King informed her.

"Are you the one that has a honey contract with the railroad?"

Alex inspected a round, light green melon. "What's a honey contract?"

"They let you set up first in a prime location and give you water and wood. Daddy says widows are good at gettin' honey contracts."

"What is that supposed to mean?" Alex asked.

"It means you're lucky, that's all," she replied.

"Our daddy was an engineer. He was killed at a washout at Nine Mile Bridge in Wyoming," King explained.

"Was your daddy Napoleon Hopewell?" she asked.

King's eyes grew big. "Yeah. Have you heard of him?"

"Ever'one in the railroad camps has heard of him. They say he saved the lives of his whole crew but lost his own. I thought maybe he was just a legend."

"No, he's real. I mean, he was real," King added.

She held out her thin hand. "I'm Lucy Springs."

"I'm Alex Hopewell. This is my little brother Darius."

"But everyone calls me King."

"Why is that?"

"'Cause I'm the king at eatin' doughnuts."

When she smiled, two dimples appeared on each of her thin cheeks. "Yes, I can see you do enjoy your doughnuts."

"My mother says I'm pleasantly chunky."

"And I'm unpleasantly skinny, but it's not because I don't eat."

"I, eh, think you look fine," Alex mumbled.

"My goodness, King, I believe big brother is blushing."

"Nah, it's just the stove. We've got our cookstove right inside the tent. It makes us all pink."

"I have a brother named Trevor, but I don't know where he is," she said.

"Yeah, we have a brother Cyrus who's wanderin' around here someplace," Alex replied.

"My brother took off from camp five years ago, and we haven't seen him since."

"Was he goin' to get water?" King asked.

"No, he was runnin' away from the marshal, I reckon."

"Do you really have some oranges back there?" Alex pressed.

"Yes, but you can't afford them," she declared.

"How do you know I can't afford them?"

"'Cause they're expensive."

"I'd like to see one, please. I want to see what they look like."

"You promise you won't steal anything while I'm back in the tent?"

"We ain't the stealin' type," Alex said.

"Everybody's the stealin' type, Daddy says. That is, if they can get away with it."

"May I see an orange, please?"

Lucy popped behind the tent flap and back out instantly with an orange in her hand.

Alex took the orange and examined it. "That's nice and big. How much does it cost?"

"You can't afford it."

"How much?"

"Twenty cents."

"Twenty cents for one orange?" Alex shoved it back into her hand. "I can't afford that!"

"I told you that."

"He wants a nickel orange," King informed her.

"We don't sell nickel oranges, but we have nickel onions."

"Do you have smaller oranges?"

"I suppose."

"Can you sell them cheaper?"

"Not for a nickel."

"How about for a dime?"

"No, but I could let you have one for fifteen cents," she countered.

"Let me see it."

"It looks like this, only smaller."

"I'd like to see it, please," Alex repeated.

"Are you goin' to buy it?"

"If it's nice."

"I thought all you had was a nickel."

"No, that's just all I wanted to spend, but I changed my mind. It's for Mama, and she deserves it even if the price is way too high."

"It's fairly priced," she huffed. "Just for that I won't sell it to you at all."

Alex's shoulders dropped. "Please, I'm sorry if I offended you. I'd really like to buy an orange."

"Don't steal anything."

"We won't."

This time she popped behind the flap and didn't come back. A tall man with thick black eyebrows stepped up beside them and plucked up one of the onions.

"She's in the tent getting me an orange," Alex explained.

"They got oranges here?" the man asked.

"Yep."

"How much?" he pressed.

"Twenty cents for the big ones, fifteen for the small ones," Alex said.

"That's expensive."

"That's what I thought, but Mama wants an orange."

"I don't think you ought to pay more than a dime for a good orange," the man said.

"That was my thought too." Alex nodded.

"She wouldn't come down on the price?"

"No."

"What kind of girl is she?" the man asked.

"She has purdy yellow hair and makes Alex blush," King blurted out.

"King!"

The man laughed. "Son, don't let dual dimples talk you into spendin' too much for produce."

"I didn't mention anything about dimples," King mumbled.

Lucy popped back out from behind the flap. "Here's the . . . Daddy!"

"He's . . . your daddy?" Alex stammered.

"I'm afraid so, son."

"I feel sorely embarrassed."

"Lucy, I hear you decided to raise the price of oranges."

"We were sellin' them too cheap," she insisted.

"I'll be the one who decides that." He turned to Alex.

"This boy wants an orange for his mother. That's a dime orange, son."

"I'll buy it!"

She shoved the orange into his hand.

He handed her a dime. "Thank you, Miss Springs."

She let out a long sigh. "You're welcome, Mr. Hopewell."

"Alex!" a young voice shouted behind them.

He spun around to see his twelve-year-old brother Cyrus sprinting toward them. "Hide me quick. There's a man chasin' me with a knife!"

TWO

"You boys step inside and—and look at the oranges," Mr. Springs commanded. "I'll take care of things out here."

Lucy and all three Hopewell boys rushed inside the stuffy tent filled with crates of produce and two cots. Folded quilts and pillows with embroidered cases covered both beds. It smelled like strawberries.

Alex lowered his voice. "Why is a man chasin' you with a knife?"

Cyrus unfastened the button on his shirt collar. "He didn't like my ideas."

"What ideas?" Lucy whispered.

"On how he could improve his pea scoop."

"What's a pea scoop?" she asked.

"Have you ever seen a man operate a shell game with three walnut shells?"

She nodded her head. "And he hides a pea under one of them, and you have to guess which one?"

"Yes, well, some men aren't too honest. They have a pea scoop in their sleeve that helps them win ever' time."

"You mean, they scoop it up and hide it?"

"Yep. And then they put it under one of the shells that wasn't guessed."

"That's cheating," Lucy declared.

"Yep. This man was taking money from some Chinese men."

Alex scratched his shaggy black hair. "So you pointed out how he could steal better?"

Cyrus rocked back on the heels of his brown boots. "It was the only way I knew to tell them they were bein' cheated."

"So the man didn't like it too much?" Lucy asked.

"Shhhh." Cyrus held up his hand. "That's him outside!"

Alex leaned his head against the tent flap to listen.

"You seen some thievin' kid run by here?" a deep voice growled.

"This is a produce shop," Mr. Springs answered. "It isn't the kind of place kids come to often."

"I thought I seen him run this way."

"Lots of folks scoot through here on their way down to look at the Great Salt Lake."

"You sayin' he went to the lake?"

"No, I'm merely sayin' lots use this as a path to the lake. That's all," Mr. Springs said.

"If you see a conniving, little squealer, tell him Lester MacHale is looking for him."

"Would you like to buy an onion?"

"No, I don't want to buy an onion."

"Perhaps some snap peas?"

"What?"

"Would you like some vegetables?"

"No, I want a squealin' meddler! I'll find him too!"

Alex could hear the man stomp away.

"Thanks, Mr. Springs," Alex said as all three Hopewell boys traipsed out into the bright Utah sunlight.

"You boys watch out for that type. He's up to no good. You better stick close to home," Mr. Springs advised.

"We're just goin' to get some water and head back to our tent," Alex reported.

"Cyrus was supposed to bring the water an hour ago," King said.

"But I just thought of a hammer head with a sloping lip. When the men are driving spikes, they'll get impact even if they're a little off line," Cyrus explained. "So I went to the blacksmith's shop."

Mr. Springs shook his head. "I don't think those ol' boys ever miss with the hammer, do they?"

"Mr. Stanford and Mr. Durant might. They aren't workin' railroad men," Cyrus argued. "What if it was their turn to drive in the last spike, and they missed? That would be very embarrassing."

"Did you talk to the blacksmiths about it?" Alex asked.

"They said Mr. Stanford doesn't get in until late tonight. No one knows where Mr. Durant is," Cyrus said. "I'll check back later."

"What do you mean, no one knows where Durant is?" Mr. Springs questioned.

"His train is comin' west but didn't make its destination in Wyomin'. No one knows where it is."

"I'm sure someone knows," Lucy insisted.

"They didn't tell me," Cyrus said.

Alex motioned to his brothers. "Let's go get the water."

"We have to get some candy first," King reminded him.

"Candy?" Cyrus asked.

"Mama gave us a nickel apiece and said we could buy whatever we wanted," King explained.

Cyrus's eyes widened. "I want two-a-penny hard, wrapped peppermints."

"I'd like some chocolate," King said.

"Where's the nearest candy store?" Alex asked.

"There's a new tent on the north side," Lucy offered. "Just hike between those two brown tents and look for a red-and-white wooden peppermint stick."

With orange in hand, Alex led King and Cyrus between the tents. They had just circled a dust-covered center-pole tent when a huge woman stuck her head out. "Sonny, come here a minute."

"Me?" Alex gulped.

"Yep, come here."

"What do you want from us?"

"Just you." She motioned.

Alex handed his orange to King and went up to the woman. Only her head and neck showed outside the tent.

"What do you want?"

"Can you tie a square knot?" she asked.

"I reckon."

"Come in here." She stood back and opened the tent flap.

He glanced back at his brothers, who both giggled and watched his every step. Inside, he found the cot decorated with silk pillows, a white fluffy cat lying on top. The air was thick with lilac perfume. A rug was spread across the dirt.

The woman's white blouse had two thick strings hanging down from beneath it. "Grab those strings, yank on them hard, and tie a square knot in them."

"What are they?" he muttered.

"My built-in corset."

"I—I—I—," he stammered.

"Sure you can. Just put your knee in the small of my back and yank with all your might."

"What?"

"You heard me."

"But—but—but I don't even know you."

"My name's April. What's yours?"

"I'm Alexander. They call me Alex."

Her fleshy, ring-covered hand grasped his and shook it. "Pleased to meet you, Alex."

"Yes, ma'am."

"Alex, hurry. We want to get the candy before Cyrus gets caught by the guy with the knife," King hollered.

Alex grabbed the two loose strings, jammed his knee in the woman's back, and yanked.

"Oh!" she squealed. "That's it, honey."

"What are you doin'?" Cyrus called out.

"He's tyin' up loose ends," April puffed.

Alex circled the string into a square knot and pulled it tight. "Is that what you need?"

"Thank you, young man. Let me pay you for that."

"No, ma'am. I can't take money for helpin' someone."

"What did you do?" Cyrus asked as Alex scooted out of the tent.

"She needed me to tie a—a bundle."

"She couldn't do it herself?" King asked.

"I guess not."

"Did you see all her rings?" Cyrus asked.

"I reckon she likes jewelry," Alex remarked.

"Mama likes jewelry, but she don't have very much," King said.

"There's a jeweler in a wagon down by the Polecat Saloon that has little silver charms in the shape of a railroad spike," Cyrus reported as they trudged past the tents.

"How do you know what's down there?" King quizzed. "Mama said we couldn't go down there."

"I had a message for Thaddeus Peters."

"Who's that?" Alex asked.

"He's a railroad engine builder. The man at the Central Pacific office said he was the one to talk to about my snow converter."

"Did you find him?" Alex asked.

"No, but you'll never guess what I did see. They was chargin' five cents a peek, but I saw it for free."

"We don't want to know," Alex replied.

"I want to know," King blurted out.

"There's the candy shop." Alex pointed.

King sprinted ahead of his brothers.

"It wasn't sinful," Cyrus whispered. "It was just a calf with two heads."

King spent ten minutes making sure he had ten different flavors of hard candy. Cyrus scooped up ten pieces of peppermint. Alex stepped up to pay the short, bald man.

"You want to try the taffy, son? It's fresh."

"No, sir. I only have a dime," Alex replied.

"For ever' dime spent, you get a piece of taffy. Help yourself to one."

Alex plucked up a pink one and shoved it in the pocket of his ducking trousers. "Thank you, sir."

He carried the orange and led his brothers back to the water wagon.

"Hmmmphmmbt, chocmmmpth," King mumbled.

"What?"

King swallowed and said, "I wish they had chocolate."

"You'd just eat it until you were sick, like last time," Cyrus insisted.

"I would not," King shot back. "Cyrus, how come you got all peppermint?"

"'Cause ever' time I stop by the shop at the Central Pacific, Morton Ferrale is chewing on peppermint. I need him to look at my snow converter. Maybe a peppermint will soften him up."

Cecil was in an argument with a bearded bald man when they reached the water wagon. "And I told you, I don't have water to sell. This is railroad water, and it's spoken for," Cecil insisted.

"Are you sayin' I can't buy this water?"

"That's what I'm saying," Cecil shouted. He turned to the boys. "Alex, you and your brothers go ahead and fill your buckets."

Alex handed the orange to King and pulled out the buckets from under the wagon. He shoved one at Cyrus and filled his own from the spout.

"Them kids get free water, and I can't buy any?" the man complained.

"Move along, mister. I don't want a ruckus," Cecil answered.

"You're goin' to get a ruckus," the man shouted. "I ain't leavin' here until I get what I deserve."

Cecil threw his carbine to his shoulder. The barrel pressed against the man's temple. "Have it your way then."

"Wait! . . . My word, don't take it so personal. I believe perhaps I could get along until mornin' without water."

"Nice of you to figure that out." Cecil lowered the gun.

The man started to walk away, then turned back. "How come they get water?"

"'Cause their daddy saved my life. If you don't move along, someone will need to save yours."

As they walked home, Alex carried both water buckets.

Cyrus carried the orange.

And King ran ahead of them.

The breeze swirled a fine yellow dust into Alex's face. The weight of the water slowed him down, and he dropped behind his brothers. His shoulders began to cramp. He set the buckets in the dirt.

Lord, I don't understand why Mama, who is the sweetest woman in the world, has to work until she can't stand up just so we can survive. I don't understand how Daddy could risk his life for others and not be around for us and Mama. I don't understand how come he could work for the railroad for fifteen years, and they only give Mama $61.35. I don't know why I can't find a job that pays enough money so that Mama could just stay at home. Lord, there are a whole lot of things I don't understand. Maybe You could just school me one step at a time.

When Alex hefted the water buckets, a sharp pain stabbed his right shoulder, but he kept hiking through the tents. He had just rounded the corner by the red-and-gold

Chinese silk tent when King sprinted his way. "Alex, there's a man yellin' at Mama!"

Alex jogged, his hands now locked in pain around the bucket handles. His back cramped. He could feel tears in the dusty corners of his eyes.

A tall, gray-headed man in a stovepipe hat stood at the front tent flap. The back of his neck was red. "I'll see you in court, Mrs. Hopewell," he threatened. "The marshal will be serving you papers within twenty-four hours if that debt is not paid. I warned you."

"What're you doin'?" Alex hollered.

The man spun around. "Who are you?"

"I'm Alex Hopewell. Why are you yellin' at my mother?"

"Because she refused to settle accounts. She thinks she can cheat Tobias Rathbone & Company!"

"My mama ain't never cheated nobody in her life."

"I really don't have time for this prattle."

"Mister, get out of here," Alex demanded.

The man stood straight and stiff. "I have no intention of being bullied by a kid."

Alex marched over in front of him. "You don't have any choice."

The big man drew a small pocket pistol out of his vest pocket. "I believe I do."

"So you're the type of man who yells at widows and draws guns on kids," Alex taunted.

"Alexander!" his mother cautioned.

Cyrus leaped out of the tent and shoved an object in the man's back. "Drop that pistol! Now!"

The man looked over his shoulder. "You threatening me with an umbrella?"

"You underestimate the power of a .32-caliber umbrella-gun fired at close range." Cyrus leaned against the man. "That click was the concealed hammer."

"Wh-what click?" the man stammered.

"Where's the kidney, Alex?" Cyrus asked.

"A little higher."

"Here?"

"Yeah, that'll do it."

The man craned his neck to stare at Cyrus. "Get away from me." When he glanced back, King scooted over in front of him.

"It's called a blueberry twister," King said.

"What's a blueberry twister?" the man asked.

"The hard candy that I just shoved into the barrel of your pistol."

The man shook the barrel. "How did that get in there?"

"King just told you. Cyrus, what happens to a brass-frame gun like that when it blows back?" Alex asked.

"Do you remember No-Nose Johnston?" Cyrus offered.

The man stared at one boy, then the other. "You . . . you . . . you can't bluff me."

Alex took a step back. "Just let us stand back a bit. You go ahead and pull the trigger. The back flash won't catch his clothes on fire, will it, Cyrus?"

Cyrus stabbed the umbrella into the man's back. "It might."

"He can't use our water to put out the fire," Alex said.

Cyrus pointed to the ground. "We can roll him in the dirt, you know, if there's anything left."

The big man turned and stomped away. "I'll be back with the court papers if you don't pay up."

A red-eyed Daisy Hopewell stepped out of the tent. "You boys shouldn't take chances like that."

"He deserved it," Alex declared.

Cyrus studied the umbrella. "I told you I should invent an umbrella-gun."

"I wasted a half-used blueberry twist," King moaned. "They're my favorite kind."

"Mama, what was that all about?" Alex asked.

"He says your daddy owed him $300."

"Who is he?"

"A lawyer for a store owner in Rawlins, Wyoming. He said Daddy was gambling and borrowed $300 from the store owner one night."

"Daddy never gambled," Alex maintained.

"No, he didn't. But this lawyer says he has four witnesses, including a justice of the peace, who will testify in court that Daddy borrowed the money."

Alex pulled off his slouch hat. "I don't believe it."

"I don't believe that Daddy borrowed the money for gambling. But I believe a man can find people who will testify to about anything."

"But Daddy died almost a year ago. Why is this man just now showin' up?"

"That's a good question. I didn't ask. I was asleep when he started yelling, and it took a minute to clear my head."

"We don't owe him nothin', Mama."

"I hope not, honey. If we have a few more good days here, we can pay off some bills at home and maybe even find a better place. I'd hate to have to work this hard and then have the courts take it away."

"We'll take care of you, Mama," Alex promised. "You don't have to worry about the scalawags."

She put her arm around Alex's shoulder. "I miss him, darlin'. Oh, how I miss your daddy." She bit her lip and wiped her eyes on her dress sleeve.

Alex plucked the orange from King's hand. "Here, Mama, I found you an orange."

A slight smile broke across her face. "Thanks, darlin'. I knew you'd find me one."

"I got me some hard candies 'cause they didn't have any chocolate," King announced. "The blueberry twister is the best so far, but I stuck it in that man's gun."

Cyrus aimed the umbrella at a seagull that stalled in the wind above them. "I got peppermints. A man can always trade peppermints."

"I never thought of candy as a trade item," she said.

"I wonder if I can trade them for a trigger?" Cyrus pondered. "This umbrella would be a lot more convincing if it had a trigger."

Mrs. Hopewell sat on a short keg and peeled the orange. "What did you buy for yourself?"

Alex reached in his pocket and pulled out a pink object. "Oh, you know, some taffy."

"Good. You deserve a treat."

"Do you want me to heat some water?"

"I suppose we had better clean up. If you boys aren't sick on candy, we need some supper too," she said. "I should have had you find a loaf of bread. I just don't feel like baking. Cyrus, why don't you go get some bread?"

"Me?" His green eyes searched the front of the tent. "Eh, I think I should stay and help wash the pans."

His mother's eyebrows raised. "Oh? Do I want to know why you're tent-bound?"

"I don't think you want to know."

"Cyrus caught a man cheatin' at a shell game," King puffed.

"I suppose he's not happy with you."

"People usually like me right off," Cyrus mumbled.

"I'll go, Mama," Alex offered.

"Take some money."

"What else do you need besides bread?"

"That will be enough. We'll have stew again. You could buy a little butter if it's not rancid."

This time Alex meandered toward a large, dusty green tent, his hands in his back pockets. He had just rounded the tent peg and started to the opening when someone grabbed his arm.

"Oh, there you are!"

"Lucy!"

"Keep walking," she whispered, "and pretend that we're friends. Really good friends."

He glanced back.

"Don't look," she warned, then cleared her voice. "You promised to take me shopping and then slipped out without me. Can we look at jewelry after we get the groceries?"

"What're you talking—"

Her elbow jabbed him in the ribs.

Hard.

"Pretend," she whispered.

"Eh . . . Okay, we'll go look at jewelry." Alex tried to glance around for anyone who might be listening to their conversation. "But I told you, I'm not buying you that diamond."

This time when he peeked at Lucy, she sported a wide smile.

And dual dimples on each cheek.

THREE

The dark, dusty tent smelled of cinnamon and cloves. A Chinese man waved his hands as he spoke to a man in a white apron. His queue kept time with the tone of each word.

Alex glanced over his shoulder. "I don't think anyone followed us in." He led Lucy over to a counter made of 100-pound flour sacks stacked like sandbags.

"I told you not to look back. You could ruin everything."

Alex took his place in line behind the Chinese man. "Of course, I did."

She rolled her blue eyes. Her straight blonde hair hung almost down to her waist. "I don't know why you don't listen to me, dearest."

Alex studied a slate board that either said "dark bread .10 cents" or "dark beans .10 cents." He scratched his head. "Dearest? Just what am I goin' to ruin? What's goin' on?"

She licked her thin, narrow lips. "A charade."

"I know that much. Who was back there?" He looked toward the tent flap and watched as a short, stocky man with a flat, reddish nose wandered in behind them. "Is that him?"

She glanced over her shoulder. "I've never seen that man in my life. Besides, I didn't say anyone was back there."

Alex stiffened, but she continued to hold on to his arm. "Yes, you did."

"No, you assumed someone was back there." She studied the slate. "Are you goin' to buy cinnamon bread?"

"No, I'm not. Mama makes the best cinnamon bread in the world. We just want the stove to cool; so I'm buyin' plain bread." He glanced over his shoulder again. "Lucy, you made me think you were in danger."

"I said nothing like that." She rocked back on her heels. "I made cinnamon bread once."

"Mama puts cinnamon in her doughnuts. Some say they're the best in the whole country." The Chinese man gathered up six long loaves of bread and turned to the front of the tent. "And you did try to make me think that you were being followed."

Lucy threw her shoulders back, but her burgundy gingham dress hung straight like a sack. "I merely said, 'Keep walking and pretend that we're friends.'"

The man at the flour-sack counter waved at them and the man behind them. "Be right back, folks. Got to pull another batch out of the oven." Then he disappeared through an opening in the back of the tent.

Alex licked his dusty, chapped lips. "See, you said I should pretend."

She rubbed her narrow neck and left slight streaks in the sweat and dust. "Is there anything wrong with that?"

"Where did that guy go?" the man behind them blustered.

Alex turned back to the man whose round eyes were

covered by round spectacles perched on a round face. "To take some bread out of the oven."

"I've been here three days, and all I've done is stand in line," the man complained.

Lucy tugged at the pewter oval pinned to her collar. "Why do you put up with it?" she asked him.

"History. I'm here to make history. When is he coming back?"

"Any minute now," Alex assured him. "You came to watch history or make history?"

"Make history. I'm a photographer. I'm going to publish picture cards of this event and sell them for a tidy profit. And someday history will not be what happened, but what my pictures show happening. Remember that, son. History is not what happens, but what is recorded as happening."

Lucy chewed on her lip. "I thought photographs show what happened."

"Now that, young lady, is exactly what I want you to keep on believing. In truth, photographs show what the photographer wants you to think is happening. There's no business like it in the world. Where is that baker?"

"He'll be right back," Lucy said.

"I'm not waiting. There must be other places that sell bread." He stormed out of the tent, kicking up dust as he exited.

"He's kind of strange," Lucy murmured. "Do you believe what he said about history?"

Alex glanced down at her hands, still wrapped around his right arm. "I'm still ponderin' why you said to pretend that we were really good friends. That implies that you were in trouble or something."

She leaned forward until her face was only inches from his. "Why do you think I'm the kind of girl that gets in trouble?"

Alex tried to pull back. "Is anyone following you or not?"

She surveyed the top of the stuffy tent. "Does it make any difference?"

Sweat trickled down the back of his neck. "Sure. If you aren't being followed, there's no reason for you to hold my arm."

She grabbed his arm so tight he flinched.

The big man hiked back inside with a basket tray of bread loaves.

"Wait a minute! . . . Wait a minute," Alex gasped. "Are you saying this is all make-believe? That no one is following you?"

"Who's following me?" the baker asked.

"Oh . . . not you. Eh, her," Alex mumbled.

"I told you, I never said anyone was following me. What's wrong with us pretending to be friends?"

"I don't like being deceived," Alex huffed.

"Did you want some bread, kid?" the man pressed.

"Do you like me?" Lucy blurted out.

"Wh-wh-what did you say?"

"I said, did you want to buy some bread?" the man roared.

"Yes, sir, I do."

Lucy tugged on his arm. "Do you like me for a friend, Alex Hopewell?"

"What kind do you want?" the man asked.

"Do you like me?" she pressed again. "Yes or no? It's not a difficult question."

"I, eh, yeah . . . sure . . . I like you for a friend." Alex turned to the man. "I'd like some sweet bread."

"And I like you for a friend." She slipped her hand back into his arm. "Now when we say we're friends, we're not playing a game, are we?"

"We got some fresh honey-oat bread just out of the oven."

"My head is spinning," he mumbled.

"Then just get plain ground-wheat bread," the man suggested.

"Did I cause your head to spin?" Lucy giggled. "I didn't know I had that effect on boys."

"How much for the honey-oat bread?" Alex asked.

"Twenty-five cents."

"For a loaf of bread? The sign over there says you have dime bread."

"I'm out of dime bread."

"You don't have any bread cheaper than twenty-five cents?"

"Nope. It ain't easy bakin' out here in the windy desert. I have to charge twice what I do back in Ogden City. Besides, it's a big loaf."

Alex dug the money out of his pocket and grabbed the warm loaf. He turned to the entrance. "I've got to get back. This bread is for supper."

Lucy stumbled along beside him, still clutching his arm. "You promised to take me to look at jewelry."

He opened the flap for her, but she still didn't turn loose of his arm. "That was just a game," he protested.

When she raised her chin, her round nose was turned up. "You clearly said we were goin' to go look at jewelry, but you wouldn't buy me a diamond."

Alex waved the bread out in front of him. "Yes, but I thought you were in trouble."

"So you'll only go with me to the jewelry shop when I'm in trouble? I guess you were deceiving me. You really don't like me, do you, Alexander Hopewell?"

He shook his head and mumbled, "You wear me out."

She tugged him toward a parked empty freight wagon with all four wheels missing. "For a strong boy, you tire easy. You don't have to buy me anything—just look at the jewelry."

He tapped her nose with the long loaf of bread. "Will you promise to be quiet?"

She rubbed her nose with her fingertips. "What do you mean?"

"Can we walk all the way to the jeweler's without you saying one word?"

"You don't like my voice? Is it too high-pitched and whiny? Daddy says I have a good voice for calling for help. But I never know if that's a compliment or not. Is my voice annoying?"

"No, it's just too busy. Give my ears a break."

She dropped his arm and stepped back. "I have half a mind not to go with you to the jewelry store, Mr. Alexander Hopewell."

Alex felt a smile creep across his face.

"But I won't give you the satisfaction. You promised to take me to the jewelry shop, and we're going."

Even though Huminski's wagon-based jewelry shop was only a hundred feet away, it took several moments for them to wind their way through scattered tents and lounging men. Lucy's hands were on his right arm, the loaf of bread tucked in his left arm.

Lord, this is so strange. It's not like real life. These aren't real stores. No one really lives here. We're all hanging around for one event. Everyone is waiting, pretending they're important. Lucy pretends that we know each other. How come she wants to hang on my arm? No other girl ever wanted to do that. At least, I don't think they did. She makes me nervous, but I don't know why.

"May I speak now? We're at the jewelry shop."

"Okay."

Mr. Huminski brushed his gray hair off his ears. "Would you two like to see anything in particular? Perhaps some wedding rings?" He winked at Lucy.

"Do you ever think about marriage, Alex?" she blurted out.

Alex stared at the jeweler, then at the tall blonde girl. "What? I'm . . . I'm only fourteen years old!" he gasped. "I don't have to think about wedding rings."

"Do you know what I look forward to most about being married?" she asked.

Alex felt his face flush. He stared down at the top of his worn brown boots. "I—I got to get back to my mother." He pulled his arm away, but she continued to clutch it.

"Sunsets," she blurted out.

He stared west at the cluster of tents and the mountains in the background. "What?"

"I look forward to watching the sunset with my sweetie."

"What kind of talk is that? We shouldn't talk like this!" he stammered.

"Did I say something sinful?"

"I—I—I got to go."

"Look, Mr. Huminski has some of those little spike charms! Aren't they cute?"

"My mother would like one, I know. But I need to get back."

"Buy her one."

"Are you kidding? They cost a dollar."

"How much do you have saved up?" Lucy asked.

"Nothin'."

"What do you mean, nothing? Everyone saves a little something. I have seventy-two cents," Lucy declared.

"Mama needs it all. I don't keep any back."

"Then how can you ever buy her a charm?"

Alex shuffled through the dirt. "Maybe I can find an odd job or two."

"You'd better. How will you ever buy me a diamond?"

"I told you, I'm not buyin' you a diamond."

She scurried to keep up. "Never?"

"I didn't say never."

A wide, dimpled grin swept across Lucy's face as she clutched his arm. "Okay, now it's time to get back."

The bread was dusty, but no one cared as they huddled around the table that still held the aroma of doughnut batter and cinnamon. Daisy Hopewell sat in the only chair. The boys all used crates. "Cyrus," she nodded.

He dropped his chin. "Lord, Alex blessed this stew yesterday, but just in case somethin' unblessed snuck in overnight, we want to give You thanks. Oh, yeah . . . if You got an extra trigger and hammer around here, I surely could use one 'cause I don't think that lawyer will be so easy to chase off next time. In Jesus' name, amen." He glanced up at Alex. "What?"

"Nothin'," Alex said.

"Cyrus has very honest prayers from his heart," Mrs. Hopewell noted as she broke off a piece of bread. "That's all I ask of any of you boys."

"Mama, what're we goin' to do about that Mr. Tobias Rathbone?"

"And Company," King added.

She dipped the bread in the stew and held it above her plate. "I don't know, darlin'. When we get back to Ogden, perhaps I'll chat with an attorney. In the meantime, I don't want you boys takin' risks like you did today."

"Mama, don't tell us that," Alex requested.

"I most certainly will. I don't want my boys shot by some loudmouth phony bill collector."

"Mama," Alex said, "Daddy used to line all three of us up every time he went on shift. He hugged us and kissed us on the foreheads and told us the very same thing every time."

Daisy Hopewell covered her mouth with her hands even as the tears rolled down her cheeks.

King swallowed a big bite of unchewed meat. "He always said, 'I love you, boys.'"

"And," Cyrus added, "'look after each other.'"

Alex sat up straight. "And he always said, 'Take care of Mama until I get back.'"

She nodded and dried her eyes on her apron.

"Those were the last words he ever spoke to us. 'Take care of Mama.' So I reckon if we didn't take risks takin' care of you, we'd be disobeyin' Daddy. Don't ask us to do that."

Daisy Hopewell shook her head and bit her lip.

"Are you all right, Mama?" King asked.

She nodded her head and got up from the table.

"We didn't mean to upset you, Mama," Alex apologized.

She patted his head. "I just need some fresh air, darlin'. You boys finish eatin' supper."

Mrs. Hopewell hurried out of the tent.

"Mama was cryin', Alex," King announced.

"She misses Daddy a lot."

"I miss him a lot too," King mumbled as he shoved gravy-soaked bread into his mouth.

"Do you think Mama will ever get married again?" Cyrus asked.

"No," Alex shot back. "Why did you ask?"

"I don't know. Nester Phillips's mama married his daddy's brother."

"I'm not getting married either," King announced. "Unless she can cook doughnuts as good as Mama. Are you goin' to marry the yellow-haired girl with the orange, Alex?"

"Her?" Alex shoved his fork in the stew. "Why did you say that?"

"I don't know."

"It was a childish thing to say."

"I'm only ten."

"And I'm only fourteen. I don't need to think about gettin' married."

"Me either," Cyrus chimed in. "But if I did, her daddy would have to own a steel mill."

"Why?" Alex quizzed.

"It's the future," Cyrus announced. "I heard they're

goin' to pull up these iron rails just as soon as they get enough steel ones sent over here from Europe."

"Why don't we make our own steel here in America?" King asked.

"That's my point." Cyrus plunged his knife into the gravy. "The future is in steel."

"Hoppy Timmins got caught for stealin', and he don't have much future," King giggled.

"You can laugh at me, but steel is the future, and someday you'll wish you had listened to me."

"The next time I have $1,000 in my pocket, you can invest it in steel for me," Alex offered.

"$1,000?" King gulped. "I don't reckon there's that much money in all of Utah."

"I bet Mr. Stanford has that much in his poke right now," Cyrus declared.

"Mr. Mudd said he once had 100 cash dollars," King blurted out between bites. "But sometimes he tells stretchers. I wonder how many pieces of candy I could buy with $100?"

"If I had $100, I'd use it to file patent papers on my snow converter," Cyrus declared. "How about you, Alex? What would you do with $100?"

Alex closed his eyes. "I reckon I'd buy Mama a first-class ticket on the train to California."

"Does that cost $100?" King asked.

Alex pulled off another chunk of stiff bread. "From Omaha to San Francisco, if you go express and first class. I would think Ogden City to San Francisco would be half that."

King's eyes widened. "On one of them fancy Pullman cars?"

"Daddy said they was like ridin' in a palace," Cyrus added.

Alex shook his head. "Wouldn't that be fine—Mama ridin' in something like that?"

"What about us?" King demanded. "She ain't goin' to leave us behind."

"We can ride the coach. I bet we could all go to California on the train for $100," Alex declared.

"Can you really get there in two days from Ogden?" King queried.

"Yep," Alex asserted. "If the snow ain't closed the passes in the Sierras."

"They would never be closed if they had my snow converter," Cyrus bragged.

"Are you goin' to eat that lump?" King pointed to a gravy-covered bite on Alex's plate.

"I intend to. Why? Did you want it?"

"Thanks!" King speared the morsel and plopped it into his mouth. Then he made a wild grimace. "It's a turnip!" he squeaked.

"What did you think it was?"

"Meat," King muttered. "Give me that bread."

A commotion outside the front of the tent sent Alex scampering.

"What is it?" Cyrus called out.

"The eastbound! The eastbound train is pulling in! Ever'one is runnin' down there."

Cyrus jumped up. "Oh, man . . . I want to see it. I need to talk to Mr. Stanford about my snow converter. His track-layin' foreman wouldn't even discuss it with me." He pushed past Alex.

"Wipe your mouth off and come on, King," Alex called.

The youngest Hopewell wiped his mouth on the sleeve of his dusty blue shirt and scurried over to his brother. When they stepped outside, the entire camp had filtered down the slope toward the western tracks. The declining sun offered a bright backlight for the silhouette of the oncoming train.

"It's a ten-wheeler," King observed. "With a funnel stack."

"It's the Jupiter," Alex said. "I thought she was parked at Reno City."

A company of armed soldiers lined the track as the train chugged closer. Alex and King stood beside a cluster of suit-and-tie men, each with a gold watch chain.

"Which one is Mr. Stanford?" King asked.

"I don't think they've gotten off yet," Alex reported. "Let's scoot up by the soldiers."

"Where's Cyrus?"

"Who knows?"

They scooted behind a long row of blue-coated infantrymen. "Do you really think Mr. Stanford has $1,000 on him?" King asked.

"I don't know. There's no way to tell. Daddy said the dirtiest man he ever saw in a railroad station owned a gold mine."

"There's some men getting off. I can't see very good. You think that's him?"

"I don't know."

"Cyrus said Mr. Stanford has a beard."

"They all have beards," Alex observed.

"That one looks like President Grant. Do you think he is?"

"No, because the president isn't goin' to be here."

"Maybe he changed his mind," King declared. "Everyone wants to be a part of history."

"President Grant already is a part of history. Besides, he wouldn't ride a train from California. He'd have to come in on the one from the East."

"Oh, yeah. It doesn't really look like him. Remember when we saw President Grant at Ft. Sanders, Wyoming?"

"Yes, but he wasn't president then," Alex said.

"Do you think any of them brought their mothers?" King asked.

"Mothers?"

"I mean wives. I don't see any ladies. Who will Mama visit with?"

"I don't suppose any of the women wanted to come out here in the desert and sagebrush," Alex commented.

"She could visit with that lady who needed you to tie her bundle," King suggested.

"I don't think she . . ." Alex paused. "You may be right. Mama is nice to ever'body."

"It's not so bad out here until the wind blows. Of course the wind blows every day."

Alex strained to peer over the row of soldiers. "I think that one must be Mr. Leland Stanford of the Central Pacific."

"I can't see anything. Boost me up, Alex."

"You're too big to boost, Darius 'King' Hopewell."

King scooted in front of Alex and then weaseled between the soldiers. "Which one do you think he is?"

"The one Cyrus is talking to, of course," Alex said.

FOUR

He liked my idea, Mama," Cyrus reported.

"You talked to Mr. Stanford himself?" she asked.

"We saw him, Mama," King reported. He leaned his head back and balanced a black checker piece on his round nose.

Mrs. Hopewell held a needle close to the lantern as she stabbed its eye with white thread. "I trust you weren't a nuisance."

Alex glanced up from a book. "Mr. Stanford didn't look bothered, Mama." He pointed at the open page. "When we get to California, I think we should raise walnuts."

"Do they raise a lot of walnuts there?" King asked as he stacked a second checker on his nose.

"No," Alex replied. "That's my point. We could be the first to have a grove."

"There's always a demand for walnuts in baking, but California sounds like a dream," Mrs. Hopewell murmured. "First, we need to witness history tomorrow and then go back and pay some debts in Ogden."

"Are you still worried about Mr. Rathbone?" Alex questioned.

"I suppose so. I wish he would just go away."

Cyrus paced around the room and waved his hands in front of him. "Mr. Stanford said water recovery wasn't crucial, but if the steam could be utilized to help melt the snow off the tracks in front of the engine, he was all for it. He said I should talk to Samuel S. Montague."

King stacked a third checker piece on his nose. "Who's he?"

"The chief engineer who laid out the whole Central Pacific," Cyrus reported.

"I thought that was Theodore Judd." King reached for another checker piece.

"Mr. Judd died six years ago," Alex reported.

With the fourth checker piece in place, King grasped for another. "But I read it at school last fall."

"Schoolbooks are sometimes out of date," Alex said. He held up the book. "Did you know that you plant walnut trees in thirty-foot diamond patterns?"

"Which book are you reading?" Mrs. Hopewell asked.

"*Learning from the Fathers: Primitive Farming at California Missions* by Professor Longview Sanchez."

King balanced another checker piece on his nose. "Where did you get that book?"

"Someone threw it away in the dump back of camp."

"No wonder they threw it away," King mumbled as he stacked another checker on his nose. "No one except Alex would read such a book."

"I can't imagine anyone ever throwing away a book of any sort," Alex said.

"Nor can I," his mother added. "But the old-timers on the California Trail sometimes discarded almost everything to make it across the desert and through the mountains."

"Did you see that wagon train pull through this mornin'?" Cyrus questioned. "It might be the last wagon train ever! The railroad will change everything."

"The rest of us were workin' this mornin'," Alex reminded him.

"And now you'll be able to take the train clear to San Francisco." King's eyes now crossed as he studied the checkers on his nose.

"I hear the last part of the trip is by steamboat from Sacramento," Cyrus corrected.

"That's what I meant," King said. "Hey, count them. . . . How many do I have?"

"Six," Cyrus replied.

"Is that all? It feels like 100."

"I think I'll finish this mending tomorrow," Mrs. Hopewell announced. "It's time for bed, boys."

"Can I sleep out in front of the tent, Mama?" Alex asked. "I like the fresh air."

"Not me," Cyrus said. "There are too many bugs out there."

"As long as you stay behind the barrels. You get out in front, and who knows what will run over you in the middle of the night," Mrs. Hopewell cautioned.

Alex toted his blanket out to the dirt between the tent and the makeshift shelf that served as a doughnut counter. He rolled up his socks and stuffed them inside his boots. He had just laid down in the moonlight when his mother appeared at the tent flap.

"Are you all settled, Alexander?"

"Yes, Mama."

"I reckon tomorrow will be busy again. The ceremonies don't take place until after lunch."

"If then," Alex said. "Cyrus heard that Mr. Durant's train was delayed or had a wreck or something."

"I hadn't heard that."

"I don't know if it's true."

"I'll pray that none are seriously injured." She stood for a moment and stared south where the moon caught a dim reflection off the Great Salt Lake.

"Mama, I'm sorry for causin' you to be melancholy this afternoon."

"Alexander Hopewell, don't you ever apologize for talking about what a great daddy you had. Those were tears of love. They just reminded me how much I loved him and how much he loved all of us."

"I still love him, Mama."

"I know, darlin'. And I will also 'til the day I die." She sighed, then smiled at him. "But none of that changes the fact that we have doughnuts to make before daylight. One more busy day; then we'll pack up."

"Mama, we'll get you to California someday."

"Yes, I imagine you will. We'll need to buy a good wagon. We can't go to California in a borrowed one like we did coming out here."

"We are goin' to get you on the railroad train to California," Alex insisted.

"Now, young Mr. Hopewell, you just keep that pretty dream. But get some rest. I can't get along without my Alex."

"Night, Mama."

"G'night, darlin'. Say your prayers."

"I will."

The stars dimmed as the moon brightened. The railroad camp at Promontory Point hummed as if every conversation was blanketed. Alex heard lots of voices but no words.

I'm tired, Lord. I'm so busy during the day that I forget how tired I am. Mama's tired too. I can see it in her eyes. Daddy always said that Mama's green eyes shone. But her eyes don't shine anymore. Not even when she's laughing. If I could buy her one of those silver charms, I bet her eyes would shine. For a minute anyway.

I wonder if my eyes ever shine?

How does a person know?

They wouldn't shine if I stared at them in a mirror; so I reckon I'd have to wait until someone told me. But I can't ask them 'cause then they would stare at my eyes, and I'd feel self-conscious, and my eyes would reflect it.

Lucy has shinin' eyes when she teases me. And pretty dimples. But I don't reckon I should tell her that. She would embarrass me something fierce. I don't know why she likes to embarrass me. It'll only be for another day or so 'cause we'll go home, and she'll go home.

But I don't even know where she lives. Must be California. They have California produce. But if they lived in California, why would they come way out here to Utah?

Lord, I don't know why I'm thinkin' of her.

She does have purdy dimples. I never knew a girl who had two dimples on each cheek.

"Hey!" The voice was a soft whisper.

Alex sat straight up on his blanket. "Lucy, what're you doin' here?"

"I couldn't sleep. It's too noisy over there. Can I sit with you?"

"But . . . I'm in bed."

"You are not. You're sittin' on top of a blanket fully clothed."

"I have my boots and socks off."

"So do I. Scoot over so I can sit down."

Alex moved over on the blanket, his knees tucked under his chin.

Lucy plopped down cross-legged beside him and brushed her long dress down to cover her feet. "Did I interrupt a nice dream?"

"I, eh, wasn't really asleep."

". . . thought maybe you were dreamin'."

"Eh, I was just thinkin' about all, you know, that we have to do tomorrow."

"Oh, good," she giggled. "I was afraid you were thinkin' about me."

Alex glared at her in the shadows. "Why did you say that?"

"Because I love teasing you."

"Why is that?"

"I don't know. I've never known anyone that I like to tease better than you. I mean that as a compliment."

"Am I supposed to thank you for teasing me?"

"I don't need any thanks. Alex, do you have a girl-friend at home?"

"What? I—I . . ."

"Tish, tish, tish. You're so shy. It's just a yes or no question. You act like no one has ever asked you that before."

"No, I don't have a girlfriend at home. Eh . . . do you?" he stammered.

"Yes, I do."

His shoulders slumped. "Really?"

"Yes. Her name is Alicen. Isn't that a pretty name?"

"You know perfectly well what I meant."

"Oh, you wanted to ask me if I have a boyfriend at home?"

"Yeah," Alex murmured.

"Go ahead and ask me."

"What?"

"If you want an answer, you have to ask me a question."

"You already know the question," Alex fussed.

"I want to hear you say it."

"Lucy, why do you torment me like this?"

"So I can see your eyes shine," she replied.

"But it's dark."

"I know when your eyes are shinin'. I can hear it in your voice," Lucy declared.

He was silent for a moment. "Lucy, do you have a boyfriend at home?"

"No. Why do you ask? Are you volunteering?"

Alex sucked in a deep breath. "What? Why—why did you say that?"

"Oh my, a flustered Alex Hopewell. I take it you haven't been around girls much."

"I've never been around someone like you!"

"Are you saying I'm special? How sweet."

"Lucy, I think—"

"Shhhhh!"

"I—"

"Shhhhh! Someone's coming," she whispered, then flopped back flat on the blanket.

The tromping of boots stopped. Alex tried to peer

through the darkness. In the shadows he could not tell if there were two or three men. He hunkered down beside Lucy.

"Which one is the widow's?" a deep, raspy voice asked.

There was an Alabama twang to the second voice. "Behind the barrel counter."

"Are you sure this is the best plan? I say we jist take 'em and ride toward Idaho. Ain't nobody goin' to follow us to Idaho."

"I didn't say it was the best plan, but it's his plan. We'll jist stash it under that center barrel. I done checked. It's empty, and the bottom is busted out."

"Why there?"

"'Cause it's the least likely place in this whole camp for anyone to look."

"I still say we should jist ride off with it."

"We don't want them boys in blue chasin' us."

"Is it really worth so much the army would chase us down?"

"He thinks so."

"Are you sure this'll work?"

"You got to take chances if you're goin' to get any-where. Ever'body will be watchin' the show. Ain't nobody goin' to be tendin' the store."

"Let's get back to Blackie's before someone spots us."

"We ain't done nothin'. Not yet anyway. Walk slow."

Alex waited several moments. Then he crawled on his hands and knees around the barrels and peeked out.

"Are they gone?" Lucy asked.

"Yep."

"Could you tell who they are?"

"No. Could you?"

"No. Isn't it exciting?" she gushed.

"They're goin' to steal something."

"Yes, and hide it right here."

"No, they aren't," Alex said defiantly.

"What do you mean?"

"I'm going to pull that barrel out and nail a lid on it. Then they have to find somewhere else to stash their stolen goods."

"But—but you'll miss the adventure?" Lucy stammered.

"I don't want that kind of adventure."

"But that won't stop them from stealin'."

"I can't stop them. I don't know who they are or what they want to steal. I just don't want it stashed at our place," Alex insisted.

"But . . . what if we could catch them? If they hide it here, we can wait, find out what it is, and go tell the army. Don't you see? We could be heroes."

"What if they catch *us*?"

"Peekin' under your own barrel?" she scoffed.

"It sounds dangerous."

"We aren't goin' to capture them. We just look at the goods and go tell the army. That's all."

"That's crazy," he fumed.

"No, it would be crazy to ignore them and not try to stop them."

"Lucy, it still sounds dangerous."

"Alex, let's make it our secret. Just you and me, okay? Don't tell anyone. We'll solve it ourselves. The newspapers will read, 'Lucida Springs and Alexander Hopewell Foil Dastardly Robbery Attempt.'"

"Lucida?" he asked.

"Yes, but I'll break your nose if you ever call me that."

"Then why do you want it in the newspaper?"

"Because it's my formal name. Newspapers are always very formal."

"I didn't know that."

"Yes, it's true." She grabbed his arm. "Alex, this is so exciting!"

He tugged his arm away from her.

"Why did you do that?" she asked.

"I reckon I've had enough excitement for one evenin'."

Lucy giggled. "So, Alex Hopewell, you find me exciting?"

"I find you confusing and exasperating and . . ."

"Exciting. Admit it—you find me exciting."

"Okay, you're sort of exciting."

"No boy has ever said I was exciting before."

"I, eh . . ."

"Now don't be so coy, Alex. You're a very smooth-talker," she giggled.

"Me? I don't even need to be here. You put enough words in my mouth, I could be in Nevada, and it wouldn't matter."

"And funny. You're quite witty. I like that in a boy. You're nothing like Hubert."

"Who in the world is Hubert?"

"Oh, so you're jealous."

"Jealous? I don't even know what's goin' on. This is like a bad dream."

"Alex Hopewell, you were dreamin' of me when I walked up, and now you are still in a dream."

"I wasn't dreamin' about you."

"Who were you dreamin' of?"

"I wasn't dreamin'. I was just ponderin'."

"And who were you ponderin'?"

"Eh . . . you, sort of."

"I knew it." Lucy leaned over and kissed his cheek. Then she jumped to her feet.

He brushed his cheek and struggled to stand. "Why did you do that?"

"Why, Alexander Hopeless, you're so irresistible when you're coy. Bye. I'll see you in the mornin'."

Then she was gone.

Alex collapsed on the wool blanket.

"Is your company gone?" his mother called out from inside the tent.

"Yes, Mama. I'm sorry. I didn't know we were disturbing you."

"That's all right, honey. I couldn't hear what you were talking about. Was it the Springs girl?"

"Yes, Mama."

"What did she want, honey?"

"I don't have any idea, Mama."

"I do," she replied. "Now get some sleep."

Alex tried to close his eyes, but every time he did, they flipped open. He stared at the stars that shone down on the Utah Plains. *Lord, this is like readin' a book with me in it. Someone else is writin' the story.*

Maybe that's the way life always is.

You are the Someone writin' our stories.

*But right now it seems like Lucida Springs is writin'
lots of it.*

*Lord, if Mama hadn't asked for an orange, I wouldn't
have gone to that produce stand, and I'd never have met
Lucy. I'd be lying out here sound asleep dreamin' of . . .
of doughnuts . . . and witnessing history. Just like that, people change our lives, even when we don't plan on 'em bein'
changed. In two days we won't see each other again; yet
my life will be different.*

*I'm glad You have it all under control 'cause I surely
can't figure it out.*

Alex stared at the stars for what seemed like an
hour.

I've never met anyone like Lucy.

Sometimes she scares me to death.

But . . . she does have a cute smile. A real cute smile.

Alex had his shoes and socks pulled on within moments
of feeling his mother tap his shoulder. Camp was quiet. The
air didn't taste dusty. He pulled on his ducking jacket and
rolled up the wool blanket. He could smell his mother's
lilac perfume above the aroma of the mix of flour, sugar,
baking soda, salt, and cinnamon. He stoked the stove and
got a fire going.

Mrs. Hopewell broke eggs into the black skillet even
before the stove was warm. "Get your brothers up, darlin'.
We'll have an early breakfast and get to work."

"Mama, I'll cook for the boys later if you want to let
them sleep."

Mrs. Hopewell studied the two boys at the back of the
tent. "All right, darlin'. Look at those two. Cyrus is lying

there dreaming of drilling a tunnel through the Rocky Mountains, and little brother is lost in a cake six feet tall."

"I like my brothers, Mama."

"That's good, Alex, 'cause they're goin' to be your brothers for a long time."

"I know some boys who don't like their brothers."

"That's sad, darlin'. You're goin' to have them a lot longer than you have your parents. I'll cook these eggs for you and me. You want to take Cyrus's water run?"

The buckets felt light as he swung them back and forth, circling his way through the tents and wagons. Campfires were scattered across the sloping plains. Voices were deep, almost a growl.

"Mornin', young Hopewell."

Alex walked over to the small campfire. "Mornin', Mr. Mudd."

The big man squatted by a small fire, wearing wool trousers and red long johns with sleeves cut off at the elbow. "Is your mama cookin' already?"

"Yes, sir. She likes to have two pans full when the sun breaks."

"Did you hear the news yet?" Mudd asked.

"What news?"

"No history today."

"What happened?"

"Ol' Tom Durant of the Union Pacific telegraphed last night there was a washout at Devil's Gate Bridge in Wyomin'. He didn't know when he was goin' to make it," Montana Mudd reported.

"The bridge washed out, but the telegraph line didn't?"

"I was wonderin' the same thing. Anyway, there's no ceremony today."

"When did they say it would take place?" Alex quizzed.

"Nobody knows. Tomorrow . . . maybe the next day. But it ain't goin' to happen on May 8. I reckon your mama will have to cook doughnuts for a few more days."

"We don't have enough eggs to last more than today," Alex reported.

"I'll get myself up there early then. I ain't missin' out on them doughnuts today."

Alex started to tramp on down to the tracks, then spun around. "Mr. Mudd, could I ask you a big favor?"

"Sure, son."

"If we have to make doughnuts after today, I should try to scour around fast and buy more eggs. Once everyone finds out we're stranded here a couple more days, prices will soar."

"I reckon you're right. How can I help?"

Alex bit his lip. "I ain't never asked a man this before, but could you . . ."

Mudd pulled a half-eagle, a ten dollar gold coin, out of his pocket. "Pay me back when I come up for the doughnuts."

A wide smile broke across Alex's face. "Thank you, Mr. Mudd. I just didn't want to take the time to go back and get the money."

"Leave them buckets. I'll haul some water up to your mama's place."

"Oh, no, sir. I couldn't ask you to do that."

"You didn't ask me. Now go on."

Alex took a few steps away from the fire. "I'll pay you back."

"Son, you're Napoleon Hopewell's boy. I reckon my money is safer than if it was in a bank."

None of the tent markets were open, but every time Alex called out that he needed to buy eggs for Mrs. Hopewell's doughnut shop, a sleepy head appeared and handed him a basketful. When he had six dozen eggs, he turned to the north and worked his way back to camp.

At the back of a dimly lit, dirt-covered tent he heard a man with an Alabama accent gripe, "They can't do this to me."

Alex froze. *That's one of the men who was in front of the tent last night. But I still don't know what he looks like.*

"He ain't goin' to like this delay neither," another man said.

Delay? Durant's train? Were they goin' to rob Durant's train?

"What do you think you're doin' back here?" a voice with a southern accent barked.

Alex spun around. A short, barrel-chested man with a bushy black beard glared at him.

FIVE

What's goin' on back there, Leroy?"

The man's slouch hat flopped down over both ears and shaded his eyes. "Some kid's stealin' eggs."

Alex stepped back and rammed his heel into a tent peg behind him. "I didn't steal these."

The voice from inside the tent was deep, demanding. "Did he hear us talkin'?"

"I got to go." Alex turned and stepped around the tent peg. "My mama's waitin' for these eggs."

Leroy grabbed his arm. "No mama needs that many eggs."

When Alex yanked his arm, the man gripped tighter. "Mine does. She's in the doughnut business. She needs 'em for cookin'."

Leroy smelled of sweat and tobacco. He loosed his grip. "Has she got that doughnut tent up there?"

"Yes."

"Did you hear that, George?"

"Let him go, Leroy," George called out from inside the tent. "I stole an egg or two when I was a kid."

Alex glanced down at the baskets. "I didn't steal 'em," he muttered.

Leroy rubbed a crumb-filled bushy black beard. "Your mama's got good doughnuts, I hear."

Alex studied the navy revolver stuck in the man's belt. "Yes, sir."

"We just might come up and see you." Leroy pushed his hat back.

Alex peered into his narrow brown eyes. "The doughnuts are ten cents each."

A big, yellow-toothed grin broke across the man's leather-tough, tanned face. "That's steep for a doughnut, but I reckon we can pay that, can't we, George?"

"Yep."

Alex didn't look back as he scurried between the tents. The morning air felt cold on his sweaty forehead. Cyrus sat outside the tent visiting with Montana Mudd.

"I see you got them eggs," Mudd said.

"Yes, sir. I'll go get your money."

"I ain't waitin' for that. I'm waitin' for the first pan of doughnuts. Fetch the money whenever convenient. I figure it's safer with your mama than in my pocket. Besides, Cyrus and me is havin' a very interesting conversation. Your brother's got a good idea."

"Which idea is that?"

Cyrus began to pace. "I was tellin' Mr. Mudd about my B.L.T."

"B.L.T.?" Alex asked.

"Beaver Live Trap system." Cyrus waved his hands in the air. "The pelts turn out perfect."

Alex eased the baskets onto the plank-and-barrel shelf and pulled off his hat. "I hadn't heard of that one. I thought you were building a rat trap."

Cyrus extended his hands wide. "Yeah, well, it's like that, only bigger."

Alex left his hat on the planks and grabbed the baskets. He pushed inside the tent to find his mother pinching balls of dough and widening the holes.

"Did Mr. Mudd tell you where I was?" he asked.

Mrs. Hopewell flashed a grin. "He said you were buying a corner on the egg market."

"Do you think I should have?"

"We would be out of eggs by noon if you hadn't. Looks like we have another day or two of cooking out of this tent."

"I hope that's okay. We do make a tidy profit."

"And you're becoming a very shrewd businessman, Alex Hopewell."

By the time the sun peeked over the distant Wasatch Mountains, four dozen doughnuts had been consumed. Sixteen men waited in line for the next batch.

Mrs. Hopewell stuck her head out of the tent. "Alex, have you seen Cyrus?"

"He went to get water."

"That was forty-five minutes ago."

"He needs to sneak around so Mr. Lester MacHale won't catch him."

"Who?"

"Never mind," Alex mumbled. "You want me to go fetch him?"

"No, darlin', I need you here. Do you think I should send Darius after him?"

"I don't think so. Ever'body is jist sittin' around waitin' for something to happen. King would get distracted. Mama, I can make it down and back before the next batch comes out."

She wiped her hands on her flour-dusted apron. "Run then, Alex."

Campfires and card games filled the landscape as soldiers, railroad workers, camp followers, and sightseers lounged on the Utah Plains.

"Alex! Wait up."

It was a girl's voice with a pleasant tone.

He spun around to see a barefoot Lucy Springs trot up to him. She wore the same burgundy gingham dress she had on the day before.

"Hi, Lucy."

"Are you in a hurry?" she asked.

"I've got to fetch some water for Mama and make it back to sell doughnuts. Cyrus got sidetracked again."

She jogged beside him. "I've been thinkin' about those men last night."

"I think I know who they are. I heard some men talkin', and they sounded just like those we heard last night."

"Did you tell the soldiers?" she asked.

"No, because it's hard to prove. At least I know who to watch. One is named George, and one is Leroy."

"Will you point them out to me?"

"Sure, if I see them. But I only saw the one named Leroy. George was in the tent."

"I've been trying to figure out what they want to steal." Lucy clutched his arm to slow him down.

"Payroll, I reckon." He brushed his raven bangs back.

"My daddy was talkin' to a U. P. man. He said the

Union Pacific owed them all back wages. They didn't expect to be paid until next Tuesday in Ogden City. I don't think there's any payroll out here."

"Then there's no tellin'. There's a lot of money changin' hands around here, with a camp full of folks buyin', sellin', and gamblin'."

"But it's not all in one place," she pointed out.

"It must be valuable and fit in a barrel."

They stopped behind a brown tent to watch a noisy little white dog chase a big black one. "That dog is called Big Bertha," Lucy announced. "Do you think those men will try to steal the golden spike?"

Alex hurried on down the hillside. "Cyrus said there were two golden spikes and some silver ones too. I don't know why someone would want them. It's a cinch they aren't goin' to leave them driven into a railroad tie. . . . And what's the little dog's name?"

"The little dog is Big Bertha. I've never seen the big one," Lucy said.

When they reached the water wagon near the tracks, two armed men guarded the spigot.

"Hi, Cecil and Howard," Alex called out. "Did Cyrus get our water yet?"

"That brother of yours is a busy young man. He said he had an appointment with Mr. Montague," Cecil replied, his Winchester 1866 looped over his shoulder.

"But that was later this morning."

"The buckets are here," Howard said. "There was a man lookin' for Cyrus. Maybe they met up."

Alex glanced around camp. "Cyrus can take care of himself . . . I reckon. I'll fill the buckets and take them back."

"Alex, tell your mama we'll be out of water by midafternoon," Cecil said.

Alex scooted the second wooden bucket under the spigot. "You goin' after another tank load?"

"They got no plans for it. Ever'one was countin' on things bein' over by now."

"What're we goin' to do for drinkable water?" Alex asked.

"Don't know, son. Folks don't know how long to make plans for now that Durant is delayed."

Howard rubbed his pointed red goatee. "This your sis, Alex?"

"No, sir. . . . Lucy's my . . ."

Lucy reached over and brushed his hair back. "I'm his girlfriend."

"I'm glad someone is havin' success out here," Howard roared. "I can't wait until I get back to town. There ain't ten women in this whole camp, and you already snagged the purdiest one."

Lucy grinned and curtsied.

Alex struggled through the tents with full buckets.

Lucy skipped alongside. "Can I help? I can carry one."

"No, I can do it," he mumbled.

"So can I," she insisted.

"I said I didn't need any help."

"Are you too proud to have help?"

"A boy shouldn't make a girl do his work," he carped.

"Alex, are you mad at me?"

His response sailed out like a well-thrown dagger. "No."

They hurried through the tents without a word until Alex paused and set the buckets down.

"You didn't like me tellin' them that I was your girl-friend, did you?" Lucy asked.

"It just sounds like something it's not."

"Alex, can I tell you the truth?"

He yanked up the buckets and started back up the slope. "Sure, as long as I don't have to slow down."

She looked down at her bare feet. "I've never had a boyfriend."

"How about Hubert?" he challenged.

"So you remember his name. I just made him up."

"Really? Why?"

"Alex, me and Daddy peddle produce. We are always moving from camp to camp. I just pretend to have friends."

"There's not even a girlfriend named Alicen?"

"No." Lucy laced her fingers on top of her straight blonde hair. "Alex, just for fun, could you pretend to be my boyfriend until we have to break camp? You don't have to buy me anything. I just want to know what it feels like to have a boyfriend."

He studied her sky-blue eyes. "Okay . . . but you know . . . it's just make-believe."

"That's what I said."

He set the buckets down again and rubbed his hands.

"Are you afraid of me, Alex . . . or just afraid of havin' a girlfriend?"

He spat on his palms and grabbed the buckets again. "Yesterday I was afraid of you," he puffed. "Today I'm afraid of having a girlfriend."

"Is that progress?"

"I don't know."

"I've got to get back and help Daddy. Will you come see me after you sell all the day's doughnuts?" she asked.

"I'll try if I don't need to help Mama."

"Thanks for pretendin' with me, Alexander."

"You're welcome, Lucida."

She frowned and turned up her nose.

". . . darlin'," he added.

A big grin broke across her face.

With dual dimples.

"I'm just pretendin'," he said.

"I like the way you pretend." She giggled, then sprinted east through the tents.

Did I just call her darlin'? Mama calls me darlin'. It don't mean too much. Does it?

Twenty-three men now waited at the tent when Alex puffed his way inside with two buckets of water. Some of the water had slopped onto Alex's ducking trouser and cooled his leg.

He grabbed a pan of doughnuts and hurried outside.

King kept the stove stoked.

Mrs. Hopewell kneaded dough and fried doughnuts.

Alex sold doughnuts and scrubbed pans.

Batch after batch.

After batch.

The sun was straight above the Utah Plains when Cyrus sneaked back. The Closed sign had already been posted.

"We could have used your help this morning, young man," Mrs. Hopewell lectured.

Cyrus plucked up a doughnut crumb and popped it

into his mouth. "Mr. Montague liked my snow converter idea. He even had a draftsman draw it out. So I had to stay and tell them what it looked like. You should see the inside of his railroad car! It's like a portable office. Anyway, Mr. Montague said if my idea worked, he would patent it and call it a Hopewell Converter."

"I heard Mr. Lester MacHale was lookin' for you still," Alex declared.

"Which is a mighty fine reason to stay in Mr. Montague's railroad car," Cyrus remarked.

Mrs. Hopewell reset her thick blonde hair in combs on top of her head. "He said he would call it a Hopewell Converter?"

"Yep. Has a nice ring to it, don't you think?"

Alex toted the big pans into the tent. "Cyrus, did you know that the water tanks are empty. We aren't goin' to get any more water."

"Yep, I know that. I told Mr. Montague, and he said we can have some water from his coach."

"You asked him for water?" Alex queried.

"He said he'd trade us six buckets for two doughnuts."

"That sounds reasonable," Mrs. Hopewell said. "Now, young man, your brothers did your work. You help me clean up, and we'll give them a break."

"I think it's a good idea if I hang around the tent for a while," Cyrus concurred.

"I'm goin' to take a nap," King announced. "I think I ate too much raw dough."

Mrs. Hopewell rubbed Alex's wide, strong shoulders. "How about you, big brother? Do you need to rest?"

He stared down at his boot tops. "I was thinkin' about . . ."

"Visitin' a yellow-headed young lady?" his mother finished for him.

"Is that okay, Mama?"

"Yes, it is. A boy does not need to work day and night. Have fun, darlin' . . . and be good."

When Alex reached the California Produce stand, it was closed. He stalled in front of the tied tent flap. "Lucy?" he called out. He hiked around the entire tent. "Lucy! . . . It's me, Alex."

He pulled off his hat to fan his face. *This is confusin', Lord. I finally talked myself into visitin' with Lucy, and she's gone.*

"Lucy?" he called out again.

"You lookin' for that skinny, yellow-haired girl?"

Alex spun around to see a huge, fat man with a cane and long white hair. "Eh, yes, sir."

The clean-shaven man chewed on an unlit cigar. "They left."

"What do you mean, they left? Their tent is still here."

"Oh, they're comin' back. But I seen Springs load up empty crates in a buckboard and head toward town."

Alex stared to the east. "To Ogden City?"

"I reckon."

"That's a long ways away."

"Yep. Maybe he wasn't goin' that far."

"Was Lucy with him?"

"Who?"

"The, eh, yellow-haired girl with fetching dimples when she smiles," Alex murmured.

"I didn't see her in the wagon, but I wasn't gawkin' at the neighbors."

"If you happen to see her, tell her I was lookin' for her."

"Who are you?"

"Alex Hopewell. . . . I'm, eh . . ."

"Are you her boyfriend?" the man in the white suit asked.

"Yes, sir, I am."

"I'll tell her. Have you heard whether they rescheduled the track-layin' for tomorrow?"

"I haven't heard. But Mama doesn't think they'll do it on a Sunday."

The man pulled out a white linen handkerchief and wiped his forehead. "She might be right. In that case, I've got to find me some more groceries. I've been lookin' for eggs this mornin'. You seen anyone sellin' eggs?"

"No, sir, I don't know where any are for sale."

The big man leaned on his cane and waddled down toward the tracks.

Alex stared at the front of the tent and the faded, peeling black letters proclaiming Fresh California Produce. *Lord, what would it be like to go from camp to camp peddling produce? Or doughnuts? Our place in Ogden City is tiny, but at least we have a place. I wonder if the Springs keep all their possessions in the tent? You can't have much if you have to pack it in a wagon all the time.*

Lots of folks have lived out of a wagon, but most of them were headed somewhere. I wonder where Lucy and her dad are headin'? I wonder why she took off and didn't let me know? She asked me to come see her.

I bet if I were her real boyfriend, she wouldn't ride off without tellin' me.

He turned to head back up the gradual slope to the north.

"You didn't say darlin'!" Her voice was soft but distinct.

"Lucy?" Alex gasped.

She poked her head around the tent flap. "You didn't call me darlin'."

He pulled off his hat. "I called you and called you."

"And you said you were my boyfriend, and I had fetching dimples when I smiled, but you didn't call me darlin'."

"But—but," he stammered.

She pulled her head back inside the tent.

He glanced around to see if anyone was watching. Then he cleared his throat. "Lucy . . . darlin'."

She strolled out, hair in a long blonde braid and wearing black leather shoes with the same straight burgundy gingham dress. "Hi, Alex sweetie."

He felt his chin drop. "Sweetie?"

"If you call me darlin', I can call you sweetie."

"But—but you won't answer me if I call you Lucy?"

She held her nose high. "Did you come over here just to argue with me?"

He jammed his hat back on. "Are we arguin'?"

"No, we're just pretendin' we're arguing."

"Lucy, sometimes it's hard to remember which is real and which is pretend with you."

The smile dropped off her face. "That's the way my whole life is."

"Is your daddy gone?"

"He went to buy more produce. We're just about sold out. When everyone found out about the delay, they bought up our supplies."

A field mouse darted out to the path beside them, spun around, and dove back under the dirty buffalo robe tent to the south.

"How come you didn't go with your daddy?"

"Because I promised my sweetie I'd be here." She put her arm in his.

He stared at her hands.

"It's just pretend, Alex Hopewell," she whispered. "Like a school play."

"But I don't know my lines."

"Make some up."

"Eh . . . well . . . do you want to go for a hike?"

"Yes," she grinned.

"Would you like to go down to the lake?"

"No," she replied.

"You wouldn't? Where do you want to go?" he asked.

"I'd like to traipse around camp selling oranges," she announced.

"What?"

"Daddy was being so careful with the oranges that they started to get a little soft. He said we need to sell them all today. He said you and me should hike around camp and sell them. We can have three cents of every dime we make."

"Really?" Alex threw his shoulders back. "How many oranges are left?"

"Forty-eight."

Alex gazed up at the blue Utah sky and bit his tongue.

"That's $1.44 profit, or seventy-two cents each, minus 10 percent for spoilage. We could make sixty-five cents each. That's over halfway to gettin' Mama a silver spike charm."

"Then you'll do it?" she asked.

"Sure."

"I have them in a basket."

"All forty-eight?"

"It's a big basket."

"I'll get it."

She held the tent flap open for him. The musty air inside smelled of fruit. One large horsefly buzzed around the center pole. Alex paused at the basket of oranges and looked at the cot at the back of the tent. The blankets were carefully folded back. There was a chipped porcelain-headed doll on the sheepskin pillow. A divided apple crate served as a dresser. Half of it was crammed with books. The other half held neatly folded clothes. On top was a pewter-framed photograph of a woman.

Lucy stepped up beside him. "That's Alicen," she announced.

"In the picture?"

"No, the doll. Her name is Alicen. Mama made her dress and painted her face when I was three."

"Is that your mama in the picture?"

"Yes, isn't she pretty?"

"Do you miss her?"

Lucy bit her lip. "Every day."

Alex shook his head. "I know. That's how I feel about my daddy."

Lucy walked over and picked up the framed picture. "Sometimes I think it's why I like to pretend so much. It doesn't hurt as much as real life."

He plucked up the basket of oranges. "Okay, Lucy darlin', let's go sell some oranges."

She set the picture down, slipped her arm in his, and grinned. "Yes, Alex sweetie."

Alex and Lucy meandered from tent to tent on the Central Pacific side of camp. A Chinese man examined all forty-eight oranges before buying three of them. A big Irishman bought one and ate it, peel and all, while they stood and stared.

They waited for a break in a poker game where the men used dried beans for chips.

"Would any of you like to buy an orange?" Lucy asked.

One man neatly folded his cards and stacked them facedown on the crate that served as a table. "How much?"

"Ten cents each," Alex said.

"Ten cents? I can get two oranges for a nickel in Sacramento," he protested.

"Yes," replied Lucy, raising her thin, blonde eyebrows, "but they don't deliver them to the Utah Plains, do they?"

He cracked a big smile. "I reckon they don't. I'll take one."

"What if I only have eight cents? Will you sell me one for eight cents?" another man asked.

"Sure." Lucy's dimples dented her cheeks. "Alex, take a big bite out of an orange and give the rest to this man."

"Whoa!" the man cautioned. "I do have ten cents after all."

Lucy winked at the man. "I thought you might."

"Your little sis is quite the saleslady."

"He's not my brother," Lucy giggled. "He's my sweetie."

Alex's face flushed, and he looked down at the top of his worn brown boots.

"In that case," a third man spoke up, "I'll buy an orange too. I reckon you two is savin' up to elope."

"Elope?" Alex gasped. "I'm only fourteen years old."

"At a dime an orange, it'll take you awhile," the man hooted.

The four bearded men roared.

"He's quite mature for fourteen. Don't you think so?" Lucy pressed.

"Shoot, I figured him for fifteen or sixteen right off," one of the men laughed.

Alex trudged on to the next tent. "I can't believe you said that," he mumbled.

"Why do you keep saying that? Do I really surprise you that much?" She slipped her arm in his. "Besides, it was just a line to help sell more oranges."

"But you don't have to embarrass me."

"Alex Hopewell, did you ever notice that just about everything embarrasses you?"

"That's not true."

"Okay, I'll carry the basket and be quiet. You sell the oranges."

"What?" he gasped.

"You march up to that man over there in the suit and tie and ask him if he wants to buy an orange. I'll be quiet and not embarrass you."

"Me?"

She pushed his back. "Go on."

Alex studied the man examining a map spread across a three-legged table. Rocks held down the corners of the map.

"Mister?" Lucy called.

The man glanced up, annoyed.

"This boy has somethin' to say to you."

The man stared at them. "Well?"

Alex cleared his throat and took a deep breath. "Eh, we have some fine . . . eh . . . Do you want to buy an orange?"

"No, I hate oranges," the man growled. He returned to his map.

"See?" Alex murmured. "I don't mind sellin' if they're in line at the doughnut stand, but I can't do this."

"Mister," Lucy called.

The man looked up with a scowl.

"Oranges make a wonderful gift," Lucy said. "I bet you have someone dear who would enjoy a California orange. It would make a delightful present. These came right from the grounds of Mission Santa Clara. I picked them myself."

The man seemed to be studying her dimpled smile.

Alex held his breath.

The man tugged at his tight collar button. A smile eased into his face. "You're right, young lady. They would like an orange. I'll buy three of them."

Lucy collected the money. Alex handed him the oranges. Then they strolled toward a large tent near the tracks.

"You see, I did sell him some oranges," she prodded.

"That's because you lied. You don't know that these oranges came from Mission Santa Clara."

"And you don't know that they didn't."

"I know you didn't pick them."

"I told you I had trouble telling real from make-believe . . . Alex sweetie."

SIX

King Hopewell licked blueberry jam off the hunk of bread. "Did you know that the railroad receives as payment from the government ever' other section of land they build the railroad through?"

"Ever'body knows that." Cyrus studied the empty amber bottle. "What if I had two circles of amber and mounted them with hinges on the brim of my hat? Then when it is real sunny, I could flip them down."

"I didn't know they got all that land." King used his shirt to wipe jam off his nose. "At 640 acres a section, that's a lot of land."

Alex leaned on his elbow at the doughnut counter in front of the tent. "I reckon it makes them the biggest landowners in the country."

"Boy, I wish I had all that land," King sighed.

Alex closed the book he was reading. "Why?"

Cyrus made circles with his fingers and held them up to his eyes. "I'd call them Hopewell's Spectacular Spectacles."

King munched on his bread. "I'd plant me cocoa beans and have all the chocolate I ever wanted."

"They could come in different colors," Cyrus mused.

"You can't grow cocoa out here," Alex scoffed.

"That's okay. I ain't goin' to get all that property either. But I can pretend."

"I could have green-tinted ones for spring, yellow for summer, amber for fall, and gray for winter. Or maybe blue."

"Do you ever pretend, Alex?" King asked.

"Big brother is always so serious. He's too busy to pretend," Cyrus laughed.

"That's not true," Alex grumbled. "Sometimes I pretend I'm an only child."

King stuck out his tongue.

Cyrus kept his circled fingers at his eyes. "You'd miss us, big brother."

Alex mimicked his brother's fingers. "Yep. I would."

Like a steel pan dropped on a rock, there was a crash and rattle behind the tent. Then someone hollered, "Cyrus Hopewell, you get around here, and you come right now!"

Alex and King sprinted after their brother. The setting sun cast long straight shadows across the Utah Plains as the air cooled.

Except the air behind the tent.

"You get that trap and varmint out of here." Mrs. Hopewell pointed to a small cage.

Cyrus squatted down. "Did my M.L.T. catch a mouse?"

"Not hardly," she fumed. "Get the whole thing out of here."

"A skunk!" King shouted. "You trapped a little skunk."

Alex kept his distance but squatted down to peer into the metal cage-trap.

"Oh, boy, it works!" Cyrus hollered as he stood up. "I knew it would. He's still alive and unhurt."

"Is that supposed to be good?" King asked.

Cyrus danced around between the tents. "I bet a larger model would work on beavers too."

"Get it out of here right now!" Mrs. Hopewell commanded, her voice higher.

"I wonder how come he hasn't stunk up the place?" Alex asked.

"'Cause he can't raise his tail," Cyrus explained. "It's too small for a skunk. I wonder how he got in there? I wonder if I can patent it as a Hopewell Kindly Skunk Trap?"

"Get it out of here, Cyrus," Mrs. Hopewell repeated with steely resolve.

Cyrus sprinted back into the tent and emerged with a small ball of sisal twine.

"What're you goin' to do?" King asked.

"Tie this to the ring and drag it up the hill."

"When you open that trap, he'll spray everything in sight," Alex warned.

"I've been thinkin' about that."

"Maybe you ought to toss the whole thing into a gulch," Alex suggested.

"What? And leave him trapped? It wouldn't be a kindly trap if I did that."

"It's better than havin' him spray our tent," Alex said.

"Besides, that trap is my only prototype. I'm not throwin' it away." Cyrus tied the string to the iron ring on the end of the cage. The little skunk hissed and snapped.

"I think he's mad, Cyrus," King said.

"You'd be mad too if you were a skunk, and your

tail was pinned down," Alex laughed. "Come on, King. Let's go with Cyrus and watch the fun."

King grabbed another chunk of bread. "From a distance," he mumbled.

They trudged up the hill with Cyrus dragging the cage-trap ten feet behind them. As they rounded the last tent, a tall, thin man with his coat buttoned only at the top pulled off his hat. "You boys got a skunk?"

"Yes, sir. It belongs to my brother Cyrus," Alex reported.

"What's he doin' with him?" the man asked.

"He's takin' him for a walk. He claims the skunk needs the exercise," Alex said with a grin.

"But he's just draggin' him in that cage."

"Skunks are very lazy," King giggled.

"I've heard that," the man said.

King and Alex chuckled all the way up the hill.

"Maybe I'll call this the Hopewell Kindly Invincible Skunk System," Cyrus proposed.

Alex shook his head. "The Hopewell K.I.S.S.?"

"Has a nice sound to it."

"How are you really goin' to get him out of there, Cyrus?" King asked.

"I'm goin' to flip the latch and run. He can push the door open on his own."

"Don't run toward us," Alex warned.

"I wonder how far we have to take him to get him where he doesn't come back to camp?" Cyrus mused.

"Idaho," Alex proposed.

"They got a Skunk River in Idaho," King announced.

"No, it's the Snake River," Alex corrected.

A mile behind the camp at Promontory, Cyrus

stopped dragging the cage. "Alex, do you think this is far enough? I'm tired."

"Maybe . . . I don't know." He scanned the hillside. "How about up there by that juniper? It looks like a gulch."

"I'm pooped too. Maybe I'll wait here," King said.

"You'll miss seein' Cyrus run for his life," Alex said. He swung a wide circle around the cage and relieved his brother of the tow string.

Cyrus trudged beside Alex as they headed to the juniper. King lagged fifty feet behind them.

"Alex, what is the difference between an arroyo, a coulee, and a gulch?" King called out.

Alex glanced over his shoulder. "Miles."

"What do you mean, miles?"

"Coulees are up north. Arroyos are down south. We're in gulch country. They all mean the same, pretty much."

"So if we were in Arizona, this would be an arroyo?" King pressed.

"Yep."

"How about lettin' him out over here?" Cyrus asked. "He can run down there and hide in that tall sage."

Alex dragged the cage to the edge of the sage-littered gulch. "Okay, Cyrus, show us how this Hopewell K.I.S.S. works."

"I haven't really given it a test before. This is just the experimental model."

"King and I will go around to the other side of the gulch. Then we can watch everythin' without bein' in range."

"How come I have to take all the chances?" Cyrus whined.

"Because it's your skunk trap," King puffed as he trotted to keep up with his oldest brother.

"And you'll receive all the fame and fortune from it," Alex pointed out.

Alex and King hiked north until a twenty-foot gulch separated them from Cyrus and the skunk.

"Okay," Alex called out. "Go ahead."

"Eh, this could be a little risky," Cyrus called back.

"What do you need to do?"

"Flip up that little wire loop."

Alex held his hand above his eyes to block the setting sunlight. "Do you have to hold the gate open?"

Cyrus studied the cage. "No, I reckon he can push it open himself."

"Find a branch or something," Alex suggested.

"A branch? There isn't anything but sage and scrub juniper for miles."

"I see a twig over by that sage," King hollered.

"It's only a couple feet long," Cyrus said.

"You can outrun the skunk," Alex encouraged him. "Besides, you can run down the slope, and he'll head for the sage."

King tugged on Alex's sleeve. "Do you really think the skunk will run to the sage?" he whispered.

Alex bent down to King's level. "No. Do you?"

King shook his head.

They watched as Cyrus crept closer and closer to the cage. The skunk didn't move, but Alex could hear it hiss.

With his feet pointed down the hillside, Cyrus reached back with the stick and tried to latch on to the wire ring.

"This ain't workin', Alex."

"You can do it."

"The stick is too limp. It won't flip the latch."

"Do it with your hand."

"But—but—what if I get sprayed?"

"Then I'd suggest you don't go into Mr. Montague's coach for a while."

"This ain't funny," Cyrus hollered.

"It's sort of funny," King giggled.

"I can't believe you two would desert me in my time of need."

Alex folded his arms. "It's a one-person job."

Cyrus glanced across in desperation. "We could draw straws."

"It's your trap," Alex insisted. "We just came along to keep you company when you have to throw your stinkin' clothes in the gulch and run back to camp buck-naked."

"I'm not laughing!" Cyrus snapped.

"Flip the catch and run. We'll holler from over here and try to distract the skunk."

"You promise?"

"Go on, flip the latch," Alex urged.

Cyrus stood at attention. "*Morituri te salutamus*!"

"What's that mean?" King asked.

"'We, who are about to die, salute you,'" Alex answered.

Cyrus hunched down next to the teeth-baring, snarling, hissing little skunk. He reached back, put his fingers on the latch, took a big breath, bit his lip, flipped the latch, and scrambled down the hill.

Alex and King yelled.

The gate stayed closed.

The little skunk remained trapped.

"It didn't work," King hollered to his brother.

Cyrus spun around and trudged back up the hill. "I know I flipped the latch."

"Double-check," Alex called out.

Cyrus crept up on the cage trap. "It's unlatched."

"Maybe it's stuck," King said.

"He could open it if he wanted to. I can't hold the door open and shove him out," Cyrus declared.

"Throw a pebble at him," Alex suggested. "If he gets mad, maybe he'll push the gate open. Are you sure it's unlatched?"

"I built it. I know when it's open." Cyrus plucked up a couple of rocks. Every time he pelted the caged animal, the skunk hissed and bared his teeth but remained caged.

"This isn't working," Cyrus moaned.

"How about just leaving the trap up here tonight? Sooner or later he might try to squirm out and push open that gate."

"But what if someone steals my live trap idea?"

"It's a risk you might need to take," Alex suggested.

"They won't steal it until the skunk gets out," King called.

"I wish I had a patent on it already. But maybe you're right. Let's go back to the tent. I'll just leave it there."

Alex and King hiked around the gulch. The sun was down, the sky gray. To the south Alex could see the Great Salt Lake lying quiet, almost dead, in the high desert.

He glanced over at his waiting brother. The gate of the cage flew open.

"He's coming out," Alex yelled.

Cyrus didn't move.

"Run, Cyrus!" King hollered.

Alex and King screamed at the black-and-white animal.

The skunk spun around and lifted its tail at Cyrus.

The twelve-year-old let out a yelp and sprinted for camp.

The skunk scrambled after him only two steps behind.

Ten steps down the hillside Cyrus lost his hat, but he picked up his speed.

"I didn't know he could run that fast," King said.

Alex grabbed the twine and dragged the empty trap behind him. "Motivation, King. Sometimes we don't have reason enough to see how fast we are."

"Do you think the skunk is gaining on him?"

"I don't know. It depends on which one gets tired first."

"What're we goin' to do?"

"Pick up Cyrus's hat," Alex said.

They jogged down the slope.

Just north of the camp, Cyrus stumbled and somersaulted across the plain.

The skunk raised his tail.

A dog barked.

A man shouted.

Cyrus screamed, "Noooooooooooooooooooooooo!"

The skunk fled east, followed by the dog and the man.

When Alex and King got there, only Cyrus was left.

And the smell.

"He marked me," Cyrus hollered.

Alex and King paused twenty feet away from their brother. "Eh . . . we know."

Cyrus pulled at his duckings. "What am I goin' to do?"

"Stay right there. I'll go get Mama."

"I didn't think he'd chase me this far."

Alex studied his brother. "He was mad."

"But I didn't hurt him. It's a humane trap. Hurry, Alex. This stinks bad."

"King, you stay with Cyrus."

"Do I have to?"

"Stay upwind," Alex instructed.

Mrs. Hopewell trudged toward the boys after sending Alex to the California Produce stand. As Alex approached, he saw Lucy helping her father unload the wagon.

"Hi, Alex sweetie!" she sang out.

"Eh, hi, Lucy . . . eh, darlin'. Hi, Mr. Springs."

Mr. Springs towered above him on the back of the wagon. "Mr. Hopewell, you two seem quite chummy."

"It's just a game, Daddy. We like teasing each other," Lucy explained.

Alex peered into the back of the wagon. "Mr. Springs, do you have any tomatoes?"

"Ain't no fresh tomatoes until June. But I have a few air-tight jars of stewed tomatoes."

"Can I buy them from you?"

Mr. Springs jumped off the back of the wagon, but he was still several inches taller than Alex. "Did someone get skunked? Or do you just like canned tomatoes?"

"Cyrus got sprayed."

Mr. Springs dug through a crate. "Here in camp?"

"Just north of here. How much do they cost?"

"Fourteen cents a can, but for medicinal purposes, you can have two cans for fifteen cents."

"Thanks, Mr. Springs."

"Daddy, can I go with Alex?"

"Yes, but I expect you back here before it gets pitch-dark. None of this slippin' out like last night."

She trotted to keep up with Alex. When they got behind the tents, they saw that a crowd had gathered around Cyrus, who sat on the dirt in the middle. Mrs. Hopewell had a couple of blankets stacked beside her on the dirt. "Alex, you and King hold the blankets so Cyrus can pull off his clothes."

"What can I do to help, Mrs. Hopewell?" Lucy asked.

"Have you got some tomatoes there?"

"Some stewed tomatoes in air-tights," Lucy replied.

"Open those and pour them into this basin. Come on, boys."

"Cyrus stinks," King complained.

"He will for a long time if we don't do something about it," Mrs. Hopewell said.

Alex held one blanket.

King held the other.

Cyrus stripped off all his clothes.

Mrs. Hopewell slid the wash basin with the tomatoes in it under the blanket.

"What am I suppose to do with this, Mama?" Cyrus whimpered.

"Pretend like the tomatoes are soap and wash your whole body with them," she directed.

"Really?" he sniffled.

"Do it, Cyrus, or you'll have to sleep out here with the coyotes tonight."

His brothers continued to hold the blankets.

The crowd dispersed.

Mrs. Hopewell and Lucy returned to camp and brought back a teakettle and bucket of water.

"I'm gettin' cold, Mama," Cyrus called out from behind the blanket as they approached.

"I'll bet you are. Wash off the tomatoes with this hot water. Here's a towel to dry off."

When he was finally dry, she shoved clean clothes under the blankets. Within a few minutes, Cyrus emerged, red-stained.

"He still stinks," King complained.

Mrs. Hopewell kept her distance. "It's the best we can do."

"I think that was the world's fastest skunk," Cyrus mumbled. "I would have outrun him, but I tripped."

"You're lucky that little white dog came along," King said.

"White dog?" Mrs. Hopewell questioned.

"Big Bertha chased off the skunk," Alex reported.

After two more jars of tomatoes and another sponge bath, things settled down. Cyrus and King fell asleep after a supper of white beans and ham. Alex and Mrs. Hopewell sat outside in the dark.

"Poor Cyrus," she murmured. "He'll just have to wear it off."

"It wasn't his fault, Mama. He was tryin' to build a humane rodent trap. How could he know a skunk would cram in there?" Alex offered.

"I know—that's the way life is, Alex. No one ever expects a skunk."

"Why do you think the Lord made skunks?"

"I suppose to remind us how sweet sage smells . . . and roses and lilacs. Sometimes the contrast can teach us as much as the example."

"Is that why He allows evil in this world?"

"I think the Lord allows evil because if He did away with it, no one would be left standin'. We all have evil in our hearts. But it certainly provides a contrast too."

"Tomorrow's Sunday, Mama."

"I know. I don't really want to sell doughnuts tomorrow, but there's no church to attend, and the men will be hungry." Mrs. Hopewell studied the shelf in front of the tent. "I will miss church. It's my most peaceful time of the week. There hasn't been very much peace out here."

"I don't reckon makin' history is ever peaceful," Alex philosophized. "I'm sorry there isn't a church out here. If Daddy were here, he'd probably start one."

For a moment neither spoke.

"Yes, your father would have had a church organized and be putting up its walls by now," she mused.

"Can I sleep outside again? It still stinks in there."

"Are you going to have company again tonight?"

"I don't think anyone will want to get close to us."

Mrs. Hopewell put her hand on his shoulder. "Alex, I like Lucy. She has a very quick mind."

He stared into the dark shadows. "She surely teases me a lot."

"That's because she really likes you, Alex."

"Mama, that's just a pretend game we play."

"Alexander Hopewell, you listen to me. You treat Lucy Springs real nice. It is not a game with her."

"She says it's a game."

"Honey, don't be fooled by words. Not hers. Not yours. Study her eyes and listen to her heart."

"But we'll only get to visit for another day or so; then I won't see her again."

"Treat her like you will be friends for the rest of your life. Darlin', treat all girls like you will always be friends."

SEVEN

Alex's back hurt.

He didn't know if it was the hard dirt bed or the trips up the slope with two buckets of water, but he did know that when he lay on his stomach, his back cramped. When he lay on his back, his side cramped. He scrunched around under the Utah stars and watched thick, shadowy clouds roll across the sky.

Then he sat up and rubbed his legs.

Mama's right. It'll be nice to get back to our house. I sleep better there. Provided one of us doesn't smell like a skunk. He crawled on his hands and knees over to the tent flap and peered in. He could hear his mother's snores and King's heavy breathing. He could smell Cyrus. He backed out, sat on his blanket, and pulled on his boots.

If I could learn to sleep standin' up like a horse, maybe my back wouldn't hurt. A bright red explosion in the southern sky brought him to his feet.

Fireworks? Someone said the Chinese workers had fireworks. But why tonight? Looks like they're shootin' them off over the lake. I bet it's a purdy sight at the shore.

He glanced back at the tent flap, then pulled on his canvas jacket, and wandered through the tents.

Another burst from a Chinese rocket lit up the camp. A number of men stood in front of their tents to watch the show.

"Kind of like the Fourth of July," one called out to him.

He cut to the east past a couple more tents and tandem freight wagons that served as a dry goods store and found himself standing in front of a darkened tent. He could barely read the words "California Produce" on the side of the front flap.

I don't know why I came over here. Maybe Mama's words keep filterin' though my mind. She says Lucy isn't playing a game. Does that mean I'm really her sweetie and not a pretend sweetie? I don't even know what a sweetie is. Lord, how is a boy suppose to find out things like that? Someone should write a book on how to be a boyfriend. I like followin' instructions. It's makin' up things that worries me.

Another burst, this one green, showered the lake. He watched until every sparkle faded back into the dark, cool night sky.

"That was a pretty one."

He spun back to the tent. "Lucy!"

"Hi, Alex sweetie."

"What're you doin' awake?"

"What're you doin' at my tent in the middle of the night?"

"I was thinkin' about walkin' down to the lake to watch the show."

"And you came by to get me?"

"Well, I, eh . . ."

"How nice. I knew you'd come." She stepped out beside him.

"How could you know I'd come over? I didn't even know."

"That just proves that I know you better than you do."

"I couldn't sleep. My back hurts."

"Do you always sleep on the dirt?" she asked.

"I got a bed at home. Me and Cyrus share one. How come you're up?"

"I was waiting for you," she insisted.

"No, really."

"Alex Hopewell, I'm here awake and fully dressed because I just knew you would come over. Are you really goin' down there to watch the fireworks?"

"Do you want to walk down to the lake with me?"

She cleared her throat and stood her ground.

"Eh, Lucy darlin', would you like to go for a walk?"

"Yes, I would, sweetie." She put her hand on his arm. "How's Cyrus?"

"Stinky and asleep."

They set out in a southerly direction. The closer they got to the railroad tracks, the larger the tents. A few even had portable wood floors and partial wood walls. Customers streamed outdoors to watch the explosions.

Alex and Lucy walked along the rail as a silver burst filled the southern sky. "Here's where they're goin' to lay the last track," he said. "They've drilled the tie where the golden spike will go, but they won't drive it in until tomorrow or later."

"They can postpone it a week for all I care," she murmured.

"Not me. I want to go home."

"Daddy says we might go to Arizona next."

"What's in Arizona?"

"A gold camp northeast of Prescott."

A salty breeze laced with sulfur drifted north off the lake. The air tasted old, used.

"Have you ever been to Arizona?" Alex asked.

Lucy's bangs flopped across her eyes. "Yes, and I didn't like it."

"I ain't never been there. I've only been to Nebraska, Wyoming, and Utah. I was in Colorado for about ten minutes, but I don't reckon that counts."

Her voice softened. "Do you want to hold my hand?"

Alex felt a lump in his throat. "Why?"

He couldn't hear her reply.

"What did you say?"

"So we don't get lost."

"How can we get lost?" Alex gazed south as another rocket exploded. "It's just a mile or two of desert. There isn't even any sagebrush down that way."

"Alex, please hold my hand. I don't like the dark."

"Then why did you . . ." He gazed into her pleading eyes. Then the rocket faded, and they stood in the dark.

Maybe Mama's right. Maybe it's not a game.

He slipped his fingers into hers. Lucy's hand felt sticky, sweaty.

A golden spray exploded in the southern sky.

"Say, you two is up kinda late, ain't ya?"

Alex turned to see a big man in suit and tie. "Hi, Mr. Mudd."

"You walkin' down to the lake?" Mudd asked.

"Yes, sir."

The man strolled toward them. "Think I'll go with ya."

"Who do you think is shootin' the fireworks?" Alex asked.

"Maybe the Chinese. They have more fireworks than they know what to do with. For all I know, it might be one of their blasted holidays." He leaned down toward Lucy. "Say, you two look good all yoked up like that."

"Eh, Lucy was afraid of gettin' lost," Alex stammered.

"So you decided to hold her hand. Wasn't that gentlemanly of you? It's a good thing I ambled along, Miss Lucy. This Hopewell boy is a smooth-talker."

"It was my idea to hold hands," she admitted. "My sweetie is very shy and easily embarrassed."

"Missy," Mudd roared, "it's really a good thing I'm here."

"It's a good thing it's dark," Alex mumbled.

"Say, did you hear what happened to ol' Durant?" Mudd blustered as they hiked south.

"Who?" Lucy asked.

"He's the president of the Union Pacific, and he's coming out to drive that last spike," Alex explained. "I heard a bridge went out in Wyomin'."

"That's only part of the story," Mudd explained. "The word is he got kidnapped."

"By whom?" Alex asked.

"His own tie-cutters."

"His own men kidnapped him?" Lucy asked.

"So it seems. They claim the Union Pacific ain't paid

them since January. They won't turn him loose until they get their back pay."

An explosion in the southern sky caused all three to stop and stare.

"You mean, we could be out here even longer?" Alex asked.

When the light died, Mudd continued to tramp toward the lake. "The telegraph operator is a friend of mine. He said Durant had to wire back east for money to be sent out on another train."

"No foolin'? History has to wait for a man to pay his debts," Alex commented.

"But they say he's back on schedule. He should be here to set the rail on Monday."

"I wouldn't mind another delay," Lucy murmured.

Every explosion in the sky revealed more people hiking down the treeless, barren shore of the Great Salt Lake. Each rocket was launched by a muted explosion, like a shotgun fired under a blanket.

"I think history better happen soon," Mudd declared. "It ain't good for a camp to have nothin' to do. Men sittin' around drinkin' and gamblin' get themselves into trouble. I'm surprised that someone hasn't been shot yet or the place overrun with footpads and sneak-thieves. I'm gettin' anxious myself to shuck these nobby clothes and get back up to the high country."

When they reached the shore, a hundred men had clustered there to watch the next rocket go up.

"Who's shootin' 'em off?" Mudd asked a man in a long white linen frockcoat.

"Don't know, Montana. There's an ol' boy in a boat that's firin' them up. He don't answer our call."

"I'll bet ol' Stanford ordered fireworks. They probably didn't get word that it's been postponed," Mudd offered.

"Might be," the other man said.

Montana Mudd tapped Alex on the shoulder, then whispered, "Follow me. We could see 'em better from over there."

Like a buffalo lost in a snowstorm, Mudd plunged ahead in the darkness. Another bottle rocket flared up over the lake as they got closer to the edge of the water. Red, white, and blue sparks lit up the night.

Mudd yanked off his hat. "Ain't that purdy? Ain't no colors better than the red, white, and blue."

Lucy nudged Alex. "He's sinking."

"What?"

"I think Mr. Mudd is sinking."

Alex saw that the big trapper now stood head to head with him.

"Eh, I think you're in a bog, Mr. Mudd."

"So are you, Alex sweetie."

He jumped back toward her.

"I lost my boot," Alex gasped.

"Dad gum quicksand," Mudd sputtered. "That's why nobody was standin' over here!"

At the next explosion, Alex reached down and yanked his boot out of the black, sandy bog.

Montana Mudd had sunk down to his boot tops. "Can't believe I hiked down into this gumbo. Find a stick, boy, and pull me out. These are ten-dollar boots. I ain't worn 'em for even a year yet."

After a silver rocket flared, the night sky went dark.

"A stick?" Alex said.

"Or a rope or something."

Lucy clutched Alex's arm. "There aren't any sticks down here, Mr. Mudd," he replied.

"Quick, boy! I just keep sinkin' lower," Mudd cried. "I'm goin' to ruin a six-dollar suit. I bought this just for the picture-takin'. Give me your hand. Maybe you two can pull me out."

Alex avoided stepping back into the bog, but reached out his hand in the dark. "I don't think I can reach that far."

Lucy grabbed his other hand. "Lean a little farther, Alex. I'll hold you."

"Hold tight."

"Oh, I will. I would never let go of you, Alex sweetie."

"Mr. Mudd . . . where are you?"

"Over here, boy. Reach a little farther."

"I wish another rocket would go off so I could see where you are," Alex said.

Clouds covered the stars. Alex heard the crowd tramp back up toward the track.

"The fireworks are over," Lucy reported.

A sulfur match flared from Mr. Mudd's fingers, and Alex spotted the man only a couple of feet away from his outstretched hand.

"It's up to your knees," Alex called out.

"Ain't that somethin'? Montana Mudd stuck like a bogged down ol' buffalo."

Alex stepped back to firmer ground. "I'll run for help."

"No," Mudd hollered. "I don't aim to be the laughin' stock of the Utah Plains. Don't tell a soul. Jist help me out of here. I can always buy new boots."

"But I can't reach you."

"Pull off your jacket."

"What?"

"Toss me one sleeve. You two tug on the other," Mudd suggested.

Alex yanked off his coat. "Strike another match."

When the match flared, Alex tossed the canvas coat toward the sweating face of Montana Mudd. He caught the sleeve.

"All right," Mudd hollered as the light dimmed, "anchor yourself and tug."

Lucy sat on the dirt and wrapped her arms around Alex's legs.

"Okay . . . pull, Mr. Mudd." Alex gripped the jacket sleeve with both hands, but felt himself pulled toward the bog. "It ain't workin'," he hollered.

"Just a little more, son."

"I can't do it, Mr. Mudd. I'm losin' my grip." With Lucy attached to his legs like a sandbag, he felt the canvas coat burn through his hand.

"Just one more yank, son."

His hand burned.

Lucy held tight.

The jacket wrenched out of his hand.

"I lost it," Alex shouted.

"Ain't this a fine quandary?" Mudd mumbled.

Another sulfur match flamed up.

Montana Mudd held Alex's coat. The black sand was above Mudd's knees.

Lucy continued to clutch Alex's legs.

"What do we do now?" Alex asked.

"Run get a two-by-four. That's all I need. I've been

in worse fixes than this—like the time the renegade Apaches cornered me in Idaho."

"The Apaches are in Arizona and New Mexico," Lucy said.

"I told ya, they was renegades."

"I'll bring help," Alex offered.

"No, son," Mudd commanded. "You do it yourself. I don't want anyone ever hearin' about this!"

"What should I do?" Lucy asked.

"Turn loose of him, for one thing. Help young Mr. Hopewell 'cause I ain't goin' nowhere, I can tell you that."

Alex tugged on his boot as the match flame died.

He reached out for Lucy's hand and grabbed it tightly.

She grabbed back.

"We have to run."

"I'll keep up, Alex. But I can't see where we're going."

The Utah Plains sloped gradually up to the railroad tracks and the camp at Promontory. The heels of Alex's boots sank into the high desert dirt. When he heard Lucy breathing heavily and panting, he slowed down.

"It's okay, Alex. . . . I can do it. . . . I can run."

"Are you sure?"

"Yes."

He sprinted toward the lantern lights.

For three steps.

Then he twisted his ankle and tumbled to the dirt. Lucy's knees dug into the small of his back as she fell on top of him.

"Sorry," she squealed.

He sat up. "Are you okay?"

"Maybe we should walk."

He struggled to his feet. "Yeah, we won't be of any help if we keep falling down."

They jumped over the rails and cut in front of the Central Pacific's engine, the Jupiter.

Alex searched through the lantern-cast shadows. "Where's a two-by-four?"

"The tailgate," Lucy puffed. "We can use the tailgate of our wagon."

She grabbed his hand and led the way through the tents.

"You fetch a lantern," he instructed. "I don't want to fall down again."

Alex pulled the six-foot-long two-by-ten out of the back of the produce wagon. Lucy emerged from the tent with a lantern.

"Is your daddy awake?" he asked.

"No, he's snoring."

"Light the lantern."

It cast a golden glow on her smooth, narrow face.

"What're you starin' at?" she probed.

"Oh . . . the light . . . It sort of makes you look . . ."

"Look how?" Lucy asked.

"Eh, older."

The double set of dimples bracketed her smile. "Thank you, Alex sweetie."

He tossed the heavy board over his shoulder, and they started to make their way back down through the tents.

"Mr. Mudd is very stubborn," Lucy noted.

Alex felt the heavy board rub through his shirt into his shoulder. "'Cause he don't want anyone to know he got stuck?"

Lucy swung the lantern back and forth as she walked.

"Yes. Doesn't it seem strange to put his life in jeopardy because he's too prideful to admit he made a mistake and needs help."

They crossed the tracks side by side.

"Sounds like how a lot of people treat the Lord," Alex mumbled.

"What do you mean?"

"They think they can get along without His help. Try to do it on their own. Don't want anyone to know they've failed. Some would rather go down than admit they need Jesus."

They continued to hurry in silence toward the lake. A cool, salty breeze came off the lake. The sulfur odor had disappeared.

"I reckon I sounded a little preachy," Alex finally admitted.

"No, that's okay. I like knowing what you believe."

"You believe too, don't you?"

"We're always moving, Alex. I don't get to go to church."

"I'm not just talkin' about church, Lucy. I'm talkin' about Jesus."

"Daddy don't talk religion to me."

"I'll talk religion with you, Lucy, anytime you want."

"Would you take me to church with you?"

"Sure, but there isn't any church out here."

"A Methodist bishop is here. There are goin' to be services at the C. P. siding."

"Really?" Alex said. "Mama will be happy. Will you go to the service with me, Lucy . . . darlin'?"

"Yes, I will, Alex sweetie . . . but I simply don't have anything to wear."

"That lovely burgundy dress you have on now will be fine, my dear."

She covered her mouth and giggled. "You're even better at pretending than I am."

"Who's pretending?" he asked.

Her mouth dropped open.

"I mean," he said, "the part about goin' to the church service. I wasn't pretending about that."

Lucy bit her lip. Her voice was a soft whisper. "I know."

When they reached the edge of the lake, the lantern cast a dim light about ten feet in front of them.

"Stay back from that black stuff."

They hiked east, staring through the darkness toward the lake.

"Mr. Mudd?" Alex called out.

"Maybe we're too far to the west," she said.

"If we keep walkin' east, we'll come to him. . . . Mr. Mudd?" Alex called out again. "This board is heavy. My shoulder is cramping."

"Let's trade."

"No," he snapped.

"I can carry that board, Alex Hopewell. It's our wagon tailgate."

"I know, but I'm the boy. I should carry it."

"Let me carry one end of it."

"I said, I can carry it."

"So you don't want to admit that you need help?"

"It's not the same thing, Lucy."

"Sounds like you're too proud to ask for help."

"Grab the board," he muttered.

He eased the two-by-ten off his shoulder and let her

hold one end of it. She held the lantern in her other hand. They continued to hike east.

"He's got to be here somewhere." Alex called, "Mr. Mudd!"

"Why doesn't he answer?"

"We must be in the wrong place."

"I bet it's way on down that way," she said. "Do you think we're lost?"

"No, I don't get lost," Alex insisted.

"Never?"

"Never."

"Boy, you are stubborn. You won't admit to getting lost, and you won't accept help."

"I accepted help."

"That's true. I stand corrected. Now are we lost?"

Alex stopped to peer out over the lake.

"No . . ." He hesitated.

"How can you be so sure, Alex Hopewell?"

He pointed. "Because there's my jacket!"

EIGHT

Where is he?" Alex gulped.

Lucy held her hands to her cheeks. "He sank!"

"He couldn't sink that much." Alex tossed the board down across the sand and inched out toward his jacket.

"Mr. Mudd!" he called out.

"Hurry, Alex, that board is sinking."

He snatched up his coat and scampered back to Lucy.

"He can't sink that much," he muttered again.

"Our tailgate can. Pull it out of there, Alex."

He tugged the big board back to the firm desert dirt. "I can't believe it," Alex cried out. "I just can't believe it."

"What cain't you believe?" a deep voice boomed.

Alex and Lucy spun around. "Mr. Mudd!"

"Ain't I a purdy sight? I was down at the lake tryin' to wash off with that salty water."

Alex stared at the man. Black sand caked his suit up to his armpits and all over his sleeves. "How did you get out?"

"I wallowed around like a pig and lost my boots—that's how. I found some firm footing on the lake side of that bog."

"We hurried as fast as we could," Alex reported.

"I appreciate it. I surely don't aim to go hikin' down here at night again."

"What're you goin' to do about your boots?" Lucy asked.

"I ain't goin' back for them—that's a fact. I'm goin' back to camp and clean up." He dug into his pocket and jammed a coin into Alex's hand.

"We can't take pay for helpin' you," Alex protested.

"It ain't pay," Mudd mumbled. "If it was daylight and them shops was open, I'd buy you two a treat 'cause you're real pals. But them stores is closed; so you take this and buy yourself a treat tomorrow. Or buy yourself anything you want. It's the kind of thing friends do for each other."

"Thank you, Mr. Mudd," Lucy said.

"Now, of course, since we is pals, I'll expect that you two won't mention this foolishness of mine to others."

"We won't, Mr. Mudd," Alex promised. "Do you want to walk in our lantern light?"

"The last thing I want is someone seein' me lookin' like this and barefoot. I'd appreciate it if you trailed behind a ways so I can slink back in the dark."

They waited for several moments.

"Did he just bribe us to be quiet?" Alex whispered.

Lucy giggled. "Yes, but in a very nice way."

"I reckon we should get back."

"Can you carry the board by yourself?" she asked.

"Yep. Why?"

"'Cause I thought you might like to hold my hand."

"But it ain't dark with the lantern lit. There's no chance of us gettin' lost."

Lucy lifted the hurricane glass of the lantern and blew out the light.

Alex knew it was late when he got back to the doughnut stand and tent. The clouds had passed over. An umbrella of stars covered the night sky. He crawled around on the dirt on his hands and knees trying to find his wool blanket.

Now I'm sleepy, and I can't find my bedding. This is like one of those dreams when I have a hard time waking up. I know I left it right here on the ground behind the counter. Or did I toss it aside when I sat up? Did I put it back inside? No, I thought about it but didn't want to wake Mama up.

Alex again crawled around in the powdery dirt beside the tent.

I bet a dog or a coyote drug it off. Or a skunk. No, it was too big for a skunk. Now I'll have to explain everything to Mama. All about the fireworks and Mr. Mudd and Lucy . . . and holding hands. Well, maybe not holding hands.

Alex left his boots on and stretched out on the dirt. He turned his jacket inside out so the mud didn't show and rolled it up for a pillow.

My back hurts.

I'm cold.

I'm tired.

He thought about the dual sets of dimples when Lucy smiled.

But it's been a good night.

A real good night.

A cool, predawn breeze sent him inside. He built a fire in the stove before his mother climbed out of her cot at the back of the tent. Alex had the coffee boiling before she had her blonde hair set in combs.

"You're up early this mornin'," she said as she put on her apron.

"I was cold, Mama. So I came in to build a fire."

"Then you better sleep inside tonight. Cyrus should lose some of that odor today if we can get him outside."

"There was fireworks last night, Mama."

"You mean there was an altercation?"

"No. Chinese rockets over the lake."

"And I slept through it?"

"I didn't want to wake you up."

"I appreciate that, honey. I was extremely tired."

"And Lucy told me a Methodist bishop is havin' services down by the track this mornin' at eleven."

"Oh, Alex, that's wonderful."

"And Lucy is goin' with us."

Mrs. Hopewell folded her arms. "Hmmm, and just when did you see Miss Springs?"

"Eh, you know, when the fireworks went off."

Mrs. Hopewell began to laugh.

"Did I say something funny?"

"Darlin', someday a girl is goin' to set off fireworks in your heart, and you'll know you found the right one. But you don't need to worry about that for a few years."

"I reckon not."

"I woke up in the night and was sure I smelled spice tonic like Daddy used. I could have been dreamin', of course."

"I dream about Daddy sometimes," Alex remarked.

"Good for you. That keeps him in our life, doesn't it?"

"I reckon."

"Mr. Mudd was coming early for doughnuts. Is he out there yet?"

"No," Alex replied.

"Don't be too sure!" a voice boomed from in front of the tent.

Alex peeked out into the dark. "Mr. Mudd? Eh, the doughnuts aren't ready."

"But come in, Mr. Mudd, and have some coffee," Mrs. Hopewell called out. "Alex built an early fire."

"Don't mind if I do." The big man barged into the tent that now felt much smaller.

Mrs. Hopewell clapped her hands. "Why, look at you in your buckskins and moccasins. Are you goin' back to the mountains?"

"Soon, Mrs. Hopewell. Them store-bought clothes were feelin' a might uncomfortable." He turned and winked at Alex.

"You look very handsome in the homespun."

He pulled off his beaver cap. "Thank you, ma'am." He accepted the tin cup of coffee. "Did the inspectors come up here yet?"

"The what?" she asked.

"The army bunch. Ain't you heard about the robbery?"

Alex glanced at his mother, then back at Montana Mudd. "When?"

"When you, me, and missy were down at the lake."

Mrs. Hopewell stared at Alex. "You went to the lake?"

"There was fireworks," Montana said.

"That much I heard."

"What did they steal?" Alex asked.

"That's the funny part. They won't say."

"Who won't say?" Alex pressed.

"The Central Pacific. Somethin' was stolen that's so valuable they stationed troops around the outside of camp and are searchin' ever' tent."

"They're goin' to search our tent?" Mrs. Hopewell gasped. "But it's a mess."

"Don't reckon they give a fig for neatness. But they seemed to think that whatever they lost hasn't left town. They're inspectin' ever'thin' leavin' here and conductin' a tent-by-tent search."

"I bet someone stole the designs for my Hopewell Snow Converter," Cyrus spouted from beneath a wool blanket.

Tomato-stained and still stinking, Cyrus Hopewell trudged off with two water buckets. King ate jelly on bread and cold ham and tended the fire.

The first batch of doughnuts were loaded on the big pan for Alex to sell as a lieutenant and two privates hiked up to the tent.

"Mama," Alex called. "Soldiers are here."

Mrs. Hopewell stepped out. "Alex, give these boys doughnuts."

The officer pulled off his hat. "I'm sorry, ma'am. We have to search your goods."

"What is it you're looking for?" she asked.

"I'm not at liberty to say, ma'am."

"Is it big or small?" Alex pressed.

"I can't tell you that either."

"I don't mind you looking at anything, boys," she

offered. "I'm a little embarrassed that things are such a mess inside. But I'll be personally insulted if you refuse a doughnut."

"Lieutenant, we don't want to insult this fine lady," one of the privates declared.

A wide grin broke across the officer's face. "The boys are right. We won't insult you." He tipped his hat. "I'm Lieutenant Santee, ma'am. This is Fisher and Platt."

"We have a lot of eggs, but they were all paid for," Alex insisted. "Besides, I doubt if you're looking for stolen eggs."

While the men munched on doughnuts and looked inside the tent, Alex stepped outside and tugged on Montana Mudd's shirtsleeve.

"Mr. Mudd, can you lift up that center barrel for me?" he whispered.

"What's under there?"

"I just want to check."

Alex squatted down on the dirt as the big man hefted the wooden barrel.

He reached up inside, past the broken boards, then jerked his hand back. *My blanket? My blanket all folded nice and neat? I bet Mama did that to teach me not to go wanderin' off in the middle of the night.*

Mudd had just lowered the barrel when Mrs. Hopewell followed the men back outside.

Lieutenant Santee tipped his hat. "Thank you, Mrs. Hopewell. We didn't expect to find anything; we just have to look the colonel in the eye and tell him we searched every tent."

"It's that crucial?" she asked.

"Yes, ma'am, it is."

"I suppose we'll find out about it soon enough."

"History will record it if it isn't found. But if we recover it, no one will ever know," the lieutenant explained.

"My, what a mystery," she replied. "Would you men like another doughnut?"

"Not without payin'," Lieutenant Santee insisted.

Mrs. Hopewell could barely straighten her back when they hung the Closed sign on the doughnut shop a little before 10:00 A.M. She, King, and Alex scrubbed up and put on their hats.

"You look purdy, Mama," King announced.

She hugged him. "Thank you, baby. I'm thirty-four years old and feel fifty today. I'm a round-faced, over-weight, plain-lookin' widow who has the three most wonderful sons any woman can ask for."

"One of them hasn't gotten back yet," Alex reminded her.

"Yes, but I don't mind. He's still very stinky."

"You think he'll meet us at the church service?"

"He'd better," she replied. "Let me get our Bible."

"Can I carry it, Mama?" King asked.

"Yes, you may, but we're taking a slight detour. Big brother invited a guest. We'll have to stop by for her."

"Oh, you don't have to come," Alex offered. "I'll go get Lucy and meet you down at the tracks."

"Nonsense. We're walking right in that direction anyway."

"But really, Mama, I . . ." One glance from Mrs. Hopewell's blue eyes silenced him.

Alex led them to Lucy's tent but hurried ahead of them.

"Good mornin', Alex sweetie. . . . Why did you put your finger up to shush me?" Lucy's mouth dropped when Mrs. Hopewell and King marched up.

"She called you 'sweetie,'" King giggled.

"Eh, hi, Mrs. Hopewell," Lucy gulped. "Hi, King. Yes, it's a little game we play."

"Does he call you 'sweetie'?" King asked.

"No, I don't," Alex huffed.

"He calls me—"

"Lucy!" Alex growled.

She laughed. "Yes, he calls me 'Lucy.'" She leaned over and cupped her hand around King's ear. "He also calls me . . ."

Alex couldn't hear what she said.

King's eyes widened. "He does?"

"I think we should hurry along," Mrs. Hopewell declared. "Your hair looks very nice today, Lucy."

"Thank you, Mrs. Hopewell. I washed it and heated the curling iron. I wanted it to look nice for my sweetie, but he didn't even say a word about it."

"I think your sweetie is too busy blushing and studying the tops of his boots."

"Has he always been so bashful, Mrs. Hopewell?" Lucy asked.

"Oh, my, yes. It used to be worse."

"Are you two goin' to gang up on me," Alex mumbled.

"I'm just practicing," Mrs. Hopewell grinned.

"Practicing for what, Mama?" King asked.

"Someday all three of my boys will be married. That means I'll have three daughters-in-law. And I expect to take their sides in all matters."

A railroad tie platform served as a stage tucked up against the Central Pacific tracks. More railroad ties semicircled the stage to provide seating. The seats were not filled, but a couple dozen men stood at the back.

Mrs. Hopewell led Alex, Lucy, and King to the front row and sat down. Her full, dark gray skirt hung to the dirt and covered her lace-up black shoes. "Cyrus said he would meet us here," she remarked.

"Do you want me to go look for him, Mama?" Alex offered.

"No. I'll not have two of you miss the service."

"Is everyone staring at me?" Lucy asked.

Alex glanced around. "No one is staring at you. Why did you ask that?"

"I've never been to church before. It seems like everyone is staring at me."

"I thought ever'one has been to church," King said. "Isn't it a rule or something?"

"Not in my family," Lucy replied.

"Here he comes." Mrs. Hopewell pointed west as Cyrus, head down, hands shoved into his pockets, trudged toward them.

"He stinks," King whined. "Do I have to sit with him?"

"He can sit next to me." Alex traded places with his youngest brother.

"Good news," Cyrus announced. "The army arrested Lester MacHale for knifing a man."

"Where have I heard that name before?" Mrs. Hopewell asked.

"He has a camp reputation for cheatin' at a shell game," Alex said.

Cyrus plopped down on the bench.

Alex tried not to breathe through his nose.

"Hey, the smell isn't so bad this mornin'," Cyrus said.

"I think you're just gettin' used to it," Alex declared.

"Mr. Montague said I should swim in the Great Salt Lake. That should take the smell away. What do you think, Mama?"

"Perhaps we'll let you try. If you don't catch your death of cold, I suppose it might work."

"I hear there's some quicksand down near the lake," Lucy said.

Alex nudged her with his elbow.

"But that might just be a rumor," she added.

"I know what's not a rumor," Cyrus whispered to Alex. "I found out what got stolen."

Alex turned his head toward Lucy, took a deep breath, and then turned back to Cyrus. "What is it?" he asked.

Cyrus looked around to make sure no one was listening. Mrs. Hopewell opened her Bible and read. King leaned on his mother's shoulder and closed his eyes. Lucy and Alex leaned forward to hear Cyrus's whisper.

"The engraving plates for the Contract and Finance Company stock certificates," he announced.

"What is that?" Lucy asked.

"It's like the Credit Mobilier with the Union Pacific, but this is with the Central Pacific," Alex explained.

"I don't understand," Lucy whispered.

"Haven't you read about the scandals around the Credit Mobilier?" Alex asked.

"No. What is it?"

"That's the company formed to build the Union

Pacific. They say if you own Credit Mobilier stock, you'll become a very rich person. But only U.P. owners and politicians ended up with the stock."

"And the same is true of the Contract and Finance Company with the Central Pacific," Cyrus added. "The stock is worth a fortune, but only Stanford, Huntington, Crocker, Hopkins, and others like them have any."

"So why did they shut down camp and inspect every tent for some engraving plates?"

"Because if someone printed up phony certificates, it would be hard to tell which are real. So some people would lose tons of money, and some would make fortunes off those phony stocks," Cyrus added.

"Why were the plates out here on the Utah Plains?" Alex asked.

"I heard they wanted to send them east for safekeeping with Durant and the U.P.," Cyrus reported.

Alex rubbed his smooth chin. "Someone must have known they were here."

"How big are they?" Lucy asked.

"About like a book, I reckon," Cyrus replied. "It's got the C.P. folks runnin' around like wild men. They might call off the whole ceremony if those plates aren't found."

"No wonder they searched every tent and don't let anyone in or out without inspection," Alex remarked.

"Shhhh," Mrs. Hopewell cautioned. "Here's the bishop."

Lucy sat up and laced her arm into Alex's. The tall man with silk stovepipe hat, black frockcoat, and full beard had a booming voice. By the time he had led them in "And Can It Be?" "Lo, He Comes with Clouds Descending," "Oh, for a Heart to Praise My God," and

"All Praise to Our Redeeming Lord," over 100 men, some boys, two women, and a girl had gathered.

The bishop launched into a sermon describing the consequences of a sinful life.

The sun broke through the clouds, and Alex felt his legs, shoulders, and head begin to warm. He sat up and tried to keep his eyes open. He stared behind the preacher at the Great Salt Lake in the distance.

Then his eyes closed. His chin dropped.

Lucy elbowed him, and he sat up.

Lord, I'm sorry. I didn't mean to doze off.

He glanced around. His mother followed the text in her Bible. King slept against her arm. Cyrus's eyes were wide open, but he was lost in some wild scheme. At the back of the crowd, Alex spotted Montana Mudd standing next to another man dressed in buckskins.

And Lucy leaned forward, with mouth partially open, fascinated by every word the bishop spoke.

Alex rubbed his eyes. *Engraving plates? You could hide them anywhere. In a box or a crate. You could wrap them in a towel and bury them in a sack of flour.*

He rubbed his temple and felt dirt roll up under his fingers.

Or a blanket. In a flour barrel. They are under our barrel! That's what Leroy and George stole!

Alex poked his brother. "Cyrus, I know where the—"

"Shhhh," his mother warned.

"Mama, I know where . . ."

She silenced him with a glare.

Alex sat straight up. *Lord, I know what was stolen, who stole it, and where it is. But I'm stuck here. I mean, I want to be here . . . but . . . I need to let someone know.*

Lord, it would serve justice if You had this service end real quick. And I know You like justice.

The bishop launched into the glories of heaven, and Lucy leaned her elbows on her knees.

The bishop preached on.

And on.

And on.

If we had sat at the back, I could just slip out. But Mama would be mad. I could explain to her later. She'd understand. I think.

Like a train running out of track, the bishop suddenly shouted, "Amen and amen." He tossed his long coat over an iron rail and called for those who wanted prayer to come forward while the rest sang "Amazing Grace."

Lucy was the first to go forward.

Alex leaned over to Cyrus. "I know where the engraving plates are."

Cyrus's blue eyes widened. "Really?"

Alex scooted over next to King, who sat on his hands and chewed his tongue. "Your darlin' went forward," King said.

Alex glanced up to see Lucy on her knees, praying with the bishop.

"Mama," Alex whispered. "This is important."

She leaned across Darius "King" Hopewell and replied, "It better be."

"Did you fold my blanket and hide it under the middle barrel when I went to see the fireworks last night?"

Her blank stare revealed her. "Be still and pray for your Lucy."

All three Hopewell boys huddled near the tracks as Lucy and Mrs. Hopewell visited with the bishop.

Alex shifted his weight from one foot to another. "I know that's what is under the barrel. What else would a person hide in a blanket? We need to hurry and check it out."

"Mama said to wait for her and Lucy," King reminded him.

Cyrus stared across camp toward the tents. "I bet they snuck back to our place while we were down here and took it."

"I hope they didn't take Alex's blanket," King said.

"I don't think they took it yet. The army is turnin' the camp upside down lookin' for those plates. No one wants to get caught with them."

Mrs. Hopewell and Lucy strolled over to the boys.

"I did it, Alex sweetie," Lucy reported.

He studied her wide blue eyes. "That's wonderful, Lucy . . . eh, darlin'."

"Oh brother," Cyrus groaned. "Mama, can I run back to our place?"

"No running around the tents. There are too many tent pegs," she ordered.

"I'll go with him," King offered.

"Maybe I should—," Alex began.

His mother interrupted. "You should walk Lucy back to her tent. She has a lot to tell you."

"Mama, let me go—"

"Alex!" his mother scolded.

Lucy held his arm as they tramped toward her tent. "I decided I wanted a real faith like yours," she explained, "and I didn't know how to do it. What the

bishop said about Jesus convinced me I needed to pray."
She had just finished telling about what she felt inside as
the bishop had her pray, when a breathless Cyrus
Hopewell sprinted up.

"It's gone!" Cyrus puffed.

"They took the blanket and the plates?" Alex asked.

"They took everythin'."

"They took the barrel too?"

"They took the barrels, the stove, the tents, the cot—
ever'thin' but our satchels. There ain't nothin' left but dirt
and Mama cryin'!"

NINE

Daisy Hopewell huddled on the bare dirt next to three canvas satchels. She clutched King. Her blonde hair streamed down her tear-streaked cheeks. She looked up when Alex, Cyrus, and Lucy arrived.

"They took everything but our clothes, darlin'," she sobbed.

"Who, Mama?" Alex questioned. "Who took it?"

"They said three men in a buckboard with two gray horses."

Alex surveyed several men who watched from a distance. "But didn't anyone try to stop them?"

Daisy wiped her eyes with her fingers. "They had court papers."

"Mr. Rathbone? He can't do that. That was a lie. Daddy didn't owe anyone money. Besides, this is Utah Territory. Those papers came from Wyoming," Alex wailed.

Cyrus studied the dirt. "The wagon tracks go right back to the rails. They can't be far."

Alex waved his arms. "Cyrus, you take the westbound. I'll go east. We'll see if they left camp yet. Hurry!"

"What should I do?" Lucy asked.

"You stay with Mama and King," Alex ordered.

"I'll take her over to our place," Lucy said. "Go on, Alex. I'll be prayin' for you."

Very few worked on Sunday afternoon. The entire camp of 95 percent men seemed to be lounging . . . waiting.

Except the gamblers.

And bartenders.

And soldiers that kept roadblocks on the two roads going in and out of camp.

Alex sprinted up to the soldiers who stood in a picket line across the dusty, narrow roadway. "Did a buckboard pulled by two gray horses come through here? They stole all our goods."

Private Fisher stepped toward him. "Are you the boy at the widow's doughnut shop?"

Alex pulled off his slouch hat and held it in his hand. "Yes, sir. They stole all our goods while we were at church."

The private held his rifle in his right hand. "He showed us a court order to repossess it, son. I sure am sorry. Maybe a lawyer can get your goods back for you."

"My daddy didn't owe anyone money. Besides, those were Wyoming papers."

"They were?"

"Didn't you read them? I need to talk to the lieu-tenant," Alex said.

Private Fisher shook his head. "You can't do that. He's tied up with the colonel."

Alex paced in front of the soldiers. "Tell him I know where the Contract and Finance Company engraving plates are, but if he doesn't act right now, he'll never see them."

Fisher grabbed Alex's shoulder. "You know where those plates are?"

"Those men stole them and smuggled them out on the wagon in our goods."

Fisher trotted toward the custom railroad car that served as military headquarters.

Alex waited with the other soldiers. *Lord, I don't know for sure the plates are there. I never even picked up my blanket, and by now there's no telling where they are. They wouldn't leave them in the barrel. But I had to say something. They can't steal Mama's stove and supplies. That ain't right. I'd be failin' Daddy if I let them do that.*

Carrying his hat and sword scabbard in his hand, Lieutenant Santee raced toward Alex. "Son, what do you know about this?"

"I overheard some men plannin' to hide something in one of our barrels because nobody would look there. I was goin' to wait and see what it was. I wanted to catch them in the act. But by the time I found out what it was, they had stolen all our goods and left camp."

"Did you search those wagons?" Lieutenant Santee asked the soldiers.

"Cooking pots, pans, stove, barrels of flour—we looked 'em over. Course we had just checked them out this mornin'," Fisher reported.

The lieutenant stared down the road to the east. "When did they pass through?"

"Ten or fifteen minutes ago," Private Fisher replied.

"Take a patrol out to stop them. Use force if you

have to. The boy and I will be along. Don't tell them why we stopped them. Just stop them."

By the time Lieutenant Santee and Alex were mounted, the patrol was kicking up dust to the east. Alex rode a long-legged black gelding alongside the lieutenant. Neither spoke. They had just crossed the top of the rise when they spotted a wagon and outrider stopped near a telegraph pole.

"That's them!" Alex shouted.

As they came up, ten soldiers held those at the wagon at bay. Tobias Rathbone rode his horse straight up to the lieutenant and Alex. "What is the meaning of this? What's that boy doing here?"

"He says you stole his mother's goods," Lieutenant Santee barked.

"I showed your men a court order," Rathbone shouted.

"There seems to be some question of validity," the lieutenant replied. "We need to double-check it. I want you to return to camp."

Rathbone's gray horse danced back and forth, refusing to stand. "You can't believe a lyin', thievin' kid!"

"I can't believe three grown men would go to all this effort to confiscate an old stove, pots, pans, and doughnut ingredients and then race out of camp and be afraid of returning."

"A man's got to recoup what he can," Rathbone mumbled. "No one wants to go against a widow, but a debt is a debt."

"We left them their satchels," the man driving the rig proclaimed.

The lieutenant slipped down out of his saddle and

hiked over to look in the buckboard. "The lad says you might be transportin' other stolen property."

"You don't say." Rathbone remained in the saddle. "You mean, they stole some of these goods?"

Lieutenant Santee studied the crates and barrels in the back of the buckboard. "He says you stole an item from the Central Pacific Railroad."

Rathbone pulled off his hat and ran his fingers through his gray hair. "And just what is that?"

"Where do you think it is, son?" Lieutenant Santee asked.

Alex climbed off the horse. "In one of those barrels."

"But that flour is about the only thing of value I recovered. Are you going to bust up my barrels?" Rathbone protested.

Alex chewed on his lip. "That flour belongs to my mama anyway," he declared.

"Which barrel is it, son?" Lieutenant Santee asked.

Alex studied the three barrels on the back of the buckboard. *It's like a shell game. The prize can never be in all three. I don't know which one. I don't know that they haven't already hidden it up their sleeve, so to speak. But . . . it's never the middle one. Cyrus said it's never the middle one. It'll be the one they loaded first. They wouldn't save the prize to the last.*

"Well, son?" Lieutenant Santee pressed.

"It's the one up there closest to George and Leroy."

"It's the boy with the eggs. I knew he was listenin' through the tent when he stole them eggs," George grumbled.

"This is preposterous. I'm a busy man. I need to get back to Wyoming," Rathbone growled.

"I'm sure you want to see what's in this barrel." The lieutenant motioned to Private Fisher to unload the barrel.

When the two soldiers climbed into the wagon, Rathbone hollered to the two on the driver's seat, "Stop them!"

Leroy glanced over at George. "You didn't pay us enough money to go against the U.S. Army."

Fisher and Platt lifted the front barrel and propped it on the sideboard.

"Now what?" Santee asked.

"That bottom board is loose. Pull it out and reach up in there," Alex instructed.

Fisher stuck his arm inside. "It's a wool blanket."

"That's my blanket. Pull it out."

When Fisher unfolded the blanket, two engraving plates clanked out on the wooden floor of the buckboard.

The lieutenant stepped over to the small wagon. "I think that solves the mystery."

"I told you, the kid is a thief. He must have broken in there and stole them while everyone was watching the fireworks."

"You did a very nice job of settin' off the fireworks, Leroy," Alex piped up.

"How do you know it was me?" Leroy challenged.

"You smell like gunpowder and sulfur. Really, that last one was a perfect finale."

"You see that, George? The perfect finale. I was gettin' the hang of it at the end."

"So you created the diversion?" the lieutenant pressed.

"My word," Rathbone blustered. "My own men

were in partnership with this thievin' kid? I've never seen those Contract and Finance Company plates before."

"Yet you know what they are. Put him in irons," the lieutenant ordered.

Rathbone spun the horse and rammed his spurs into the brown gelding's flanks so hard that the horse reared up. The attorney tumbled to the ground. He lay flat on his back, gasping for breath. Alex stepped over and offered him a hand.

Rathbone leaped up, grabbed Alex by the shirt collar, and shoved a sneak gun at his head. "I'm ridin' out of here," he growled.

Alex took a deep breath. *Lord, I can't die yet. I've got to take care of Mama.*

"I want those plates," Rathbone screamed, "or I kill this boy. Leroy, you and George grab a horse and help me."

"I ain't takin' part in kidnappin' no boy. A man can get lynched for that," Leroy replied.

While all the soldiers pointed guns at the trio of thieves, the lieutenant retrieved the engraving plates from the wagon bed.

"Give them to me!" Rathbone shouted.

"Yes, I believe I will." Lieutenant Santee marched straight toward Rathbone and then sailed the engraving plates fifty feet out into the desert.

"No!" Rathbone hollered.

His scream was cut short by the barrel of Santee's revolver crashing into his head. He crumpled to the dirt beside Alex.

"Put him in irons and toss him in the wagon. Let's take the colonel his thieves, Stanford his plates, and the widow lady back her son."

"Not to mention returnin' the doughnut shop," Platt added. "Them was mighty tasty doughnuts."

Alex felt a firm hand on his shoulder. He rolled over in the lantern-lit tent.

"Mornin', my hero," his mother whispered.

"I'm not a hero, Mama. Daddy was a hero."

"And he'd be proud of you. The lieutenant came by last night after you fell asleep and said they telegraphed Wyoming. Those papers were forged. There's no such judge."

Alex sat up and rubbed his eyes. "Why did he pick on us?"

"Because no one would suspect a widow's belongings." She tied on her apron. "One more day to cook doughnuts."

He folded his blanket. "I guess I was tired, Mama."

"We're all tired, darlin'. Get your brothers up. This might be our busiest day yet. Mr. Mudd reported that Durant showed up last night. The celebration will be today for sure."

"Will we leave for home tonight?" Alex asked.

"We'll wait until morning," she replied.

"We'll stop making doughnuts to watch the ceremony, won't we?"

"We certainly will." Mrs. Hopewell set the big tin bowl on the crate that served as a table. "My boys are goin' to see some railroad history."

Mrs. Hopewell fried skillet after skillet of doughnuts in the sizzling lard.

King fed the fire and sampled the flawed ones.

Cyrus kept the pans washed and drew a sketch for a Hopewell Automatic Doughnut Machine.

And Alex sold 412 doughnuts before they ran out of baking soda and eggs.

Mrs. Hopewell stood by the counter in front of the tent and gazed toward the tracks. "Looks like the crowd is forming down there. I reckon we sold out at the right time."

"Mama, is your back hurtin' you again?" Alex asked.

"I just can't seem to straighten it up."

"Maybe you ought to lie down for a few minutes," Alex suggested.

"I was thinkin' the same thing. Why don't you take the boys and find us a good place to watch? I'll come down shortly. We can wash pans later."

"Mama, we made over $200 in two weeks. That's good, isn't it?"

"It's wonderful, Alex."

"Do you think we can get a bigger house?"

"Maybe we can. There're still some bills to pay. But right now that narrow little cot looks mighty inviting."

Cyrus ran ahead of his brothers, but Darius "King" Hopewell tagged along as Alex hiked to the California Produce stand.

"Hi, Lucy darlin'," King giggled.

"Oh, there's my sweetie and little brother," she laughed. "Are you goin' down now?"

"Mama wants us to find a good watchin' spot."

"Daddy said I could go now too. The quartermaster for the army came by and bought us out. Daddy's real happy. He said we might not need to go to Arizona."

"Where will you go?" Alex asked.

"I told him Ogden might be nice, but he doesn't think we can compete with the Saints. They only buy from each other, you know. But I don't want to think about that. He'd really like to get to California someday; so maybe we'll work our way west."

She held Alex's arm as they trudged along with the crowd that thronged toward the tracks.

"We're packing up in the morning and goin' home," Alex blurted out.

"Daddy said we might leave tonight since we're all out of everything. Alex, the past four days have been the best days of my life. And I don't mean just you. I was serious about my prayer yesterday."

"I know you were, Lucy. I've liked the last few days too. It's been like a dream."

"Are you sayin' I'm dreamy?" she giggled.

He looked down at his boot tops. "You're the best friend I ever had that was a girl," he mumbled.

"I'm not your friend," she declared.

He looked up with wide eyes. "You aren't?"

"No, I'm your darlin', Alexander Hopewell. Don't you forget that."

"I don't reckon I will." Something shiny caught his eye. "There's a dime." He stooped down and picked it up.

"Who does it belong to?" King asked.

"It belongs to Alex. There's no way of finding the owner," Lucy insisted.

Alex pulled out the other coins from his pocket. "That makes ninety cents. I wonder if Mr. Huminski will sell those little spike charms cheaper after today? I could buy one in the mornin' before we leave if he'd sell it for ninety cents."

"You've got over a dollar," King pointed out, counting the coins.

"Me and Lucy are goin' to split that two-bit piece. Mr. Mudd gave that to both of us."

"Why?" King asked.

"Eh, we helped him a little."

"Alex, you keep my part," Lucy offered.

"I will not. It belongs to you."

"I know it does, and I give it to you. That's what darlin's do."

"But I can't take it."

Lucy pulled a tiny silver necklace from the high collar of her dress. "Look what Daddy bought me."

"You have a spike charm?"

"Yes, and I insist you buy your mama one."

"Well, if that's what darlin's do . . . I guess I just might."

Hundreds of soldiers stood in a line on the north side of the tracks, guns held in white gloves in front of them. Dozens of photographers with big boxy cameras positioned themselves on the south side. From the west, the Central Pacific's Jupiter chugged forward. From the east, the Union Pacific's Engine 119 steamed west.

Mrs. Hopewell arrived about the same time Mr. Springs did. They all stood together on a knoll.

"What did I miss?" she asked.

"Boring speeches," King announced.

"And a telegram from the president," Alex added.

"Where's Cyrus?" Mrs. Hopewell asked.

"We haven't seen him," Alex replied.

"There he is," King shouted. "How did he get up on that engine?"

Alex glanced up at the funneled smokestack of the Jupiter. Cyrus Hopewell huddled among a dozen railroad men.

"He's goin' to be in the picture!" Alex exclaimed.

"Why does that not surprise me?" Mrs. Hopewell sighed. "With red tint still on his hair and smellin' skunky, Cyrus Hopewell will get his picture taken."

"Mama, I've got something for you," Alex informed her.

"Just a minute, honey. Let's watch."

The Central Pacific's Chinese crew hoisted the 500-pound iron rail in their arms. A railroad man with a round company hat halted them so that the photographers could get the best angle. With all in place, the man shouted at the photographers, "Shoot!" The Chinese crew threw down the rail and ran and hid.

"Did you see that?" King laughed. "They thought someone was going to shoot them."

"I do trust that none of them were injured," Mrs. Hopewell remarked.

When the roar of the crowd died, the official got the Chinese crew back, and they proceeded to lay the last two rails.

"Mama, hold out your hand," Alex instructed.

Mrs. Hopewell opened the palm of her left hand where the third finger still sported the gold wedding ring. Alex pulled a little cloth pouch out of his shirt pocket and placed it in her hand.

"What is it?" Mrs. Hopewell asked.

"Open it, Mama."

She pulled out the tiny silver spike. "Oh, darlin' . . . where did you get this?" Her blue eyes shone.

"I saved some money. Lucy sort of helped me."

She hugged him and kissed his cheek. "It's one of the nicest gifts I ever received."

"I have one too, Mrs. Hopewell," Lucy said. "My daddy bought it for me."

Mrs. Hopewell slipped an arm around the girl's shoulder. "Lucy, we both have wonderful men in our family, don't we?"

Lucy Springs nodded her head.

"Hey," King hollered. "They're going to drive the last spike. Which one is Mr. Stanford?"

"The one on the left, the big man," Alex answered.

"Did you know that they have a wire hooked up to the spike and the hammer, and when he drives it in, it will telegraph east and west that the railroad is completed?" King asked.

"I believe Cyrus told me about that," Lucy said.

Along with the crowd, Alex held his breath as he watched Leland Stanford raise the hammer above his head.

The hammer came down.

The photographers clicked their cameras.

The crowd cheered.

"He missed," King shouted. "He missed the spike!"

"Cyrus tried to sell them on his Hopewell Strike-all Hammer," Alex said.

"Look, Thomas Durant of the Union Pacific is going to try." Lucy pointed.

The hammer swung.

The cameras clicked.

The crowd roared.

"He missed too!" King roared. "We could be here all day. I could starve before that spike gets driven."

"They should have listened to Cyrus," Alex commented.

"I believe that railroad man just drove it in," Mrs. Hopewell observed.

The crowd cheered one more time.

And the railroad was complete.

The West would never be the same.

They still stood and watched as Cyrus tramped up with a suit-and-tie man by his side. "Hey, did you see me? I was on the Jupiter."

"Did you get steamed?" King asked.

"No. It was kind of hot though," Cyrus replied. "Mama, this is Mr. Quitley. He's a secretary for Mr. Montague. He needs to talk to Alex."

"What about?" Alex asked.

"Young man, Mr. Montague and Mr. Stanford are grateful for your assistance in recovering our stolen property. You saved the Central Pacific from disaster."

Alex glanced at his mother, then at the man. "Thank you, but it was what anyone would do."

"That's not entirely true. They want to give you a little token of thanks from the Central Pacific," Quitley explained.

"I already got one for my mama," Alex declared.

Quitley looked puzzled. "Got one what?"

"A token. One of those little silver spike charms."

Mr. Quitley grinned. "We want to give you this rail pass." He held a certificate in his hand.

"Rail pass?" Alex quizzed.

"It's good for one year on both the Central and Union Pacific Railroads."

Alex felt a big lump in his throat as he tried to swallow. "You mean, a free train ticket?"

"It's coach class. It's actually a pass for all of you."

"We can all go to California?" Alex asked.

"California or Omaha or any stop in between for a year. Now how many of you are there in your party? I need to put a number on the pass."

Alex bit his lip and glanced at Lucy. He swept his hand at those clustered around him. "Why, there's six of us here."

"Then six it is!" Quitley wrote the number on the pass and handed it to him. "I have to get back. My work is just getting started. Nice to meet you, Mr. and Mrs. Hopewell." The railroad secretary scurried back to the crowd.

"Free train pass?" Cyrus exclaimed. "I can't believe that."

Lucy grabbed Alex's arm. "And you included me and my daddy."

Alex took a big breath and for a split second, he knew his eyes shone. "It's the kind of thing sweeties do," he murmured.

For a list of other books
by this author, write:
Stephen Bly
Winchester, Idaho 83555,
or check out his website:
www.blybooks.com